Finding Her Sweet Spots

A Reverse Harem Romance Novella

Joya M. Lively

Copyright © 2024 Joya Lively

All rights reserved. No part of this publication may be reproduced, distributed, or transmitted in any form without prior consent of the author.

JOYA'S JOYFUL UPDATES:

New title updates and news about discounts are available when you sign up for Joya's newsletter.

Sign up here: bit.ly/34ajqt7

TABLE OF CONTENTS

Chapter One 1
Chapter Two 7
Chapter Three 11
Chapter Four 17
Chapter Five 23
Chapter Six 31
Chapter Seven 37
Chapter Eight 45
Chapter Nine 51
Chapter Ten 59
Chapter Eleven 65
Chapter Twelve 71
Chapter Thirteen 75
Chapter Fourteen 81
Chapter Fifteen 87
Chapter Sixteen 93
Chapter Seventeen 99

Hello Lovely Reader,

Thank you for choosing this book!

While this book has all the fun light stuff, it also includes graphic sex scenes.

If you're a numbers gal or guy, I counted how many times the word "cock" was used and it's 15. That's almost as many cock mentions as there are chapters! And it doesn't include euphemisms like length, steel, etc. So if you're not afraid of some big cock, go right on ahead.

& enjoy!

Love, Joya

CHAPTER ONE
Emily

I've worked relentlessly for every single thing I have. But the muscular thigh that presses against my own under the table reminds me that not everything is achievable. I have a good chunk of money saved, despite growing up with less than none. I have my health, while not everyone in my family is so lucky. And I'm in the graduate school program of my dreams. But what I can never have is the satisfaction that would come from finally grabbing that thigh and feeling my way up Ben's muscles and...

I sigh in frustration, stopping my mind from going there for the millionth time today. What is wrong with me today? Valentine's Day must be messing with my brain.

"Something bothering you, Em?" I don't have to look up to know the teasing look in Ben's eyes that would greet me. Instead, I let the touch of our legs linger for a fraction of a second too long, savoring the delicious warmth. Even if he's just having fun with me, I can still enjoy it a little before I pull it away.

"Alright, boys," I slam my laptop shut. "I need to end a little early tonight. I'll do a read-through of what we have tomorrow morning and add my notes."

"This is a new one. You never leave before us. Big Valentine's Day plans, Ms. Miller?" Deacon's little nickname for me never fails to get me riled up. I glare at him as I slip my laptop into my oversized leather purse. His dimpled grin melts my last ounce of reserve.

"Do you guys have some kind of running bet to see who can get under my skin quicker?" I glare suspiciously at the three of them. Deacon, Graham, and Ben Sweet are my classmates in my MBA program. The three brothers took pity on me when I didn't have a group to join in our Financial Accounting & Reporting class during our first semester. It took us all by surprise that day to learn that we work incredibly well together. We have nothing in common.

They're three huge presences in both status and stature. They tower over most of the student body, likely from all the supermodel genes running through their lineage. And their family has no shortage of supermodel genes because they're that old-money kind of rich that has buildings named after them. They own one of the oldest and largest confectionary conglomerates in the world. Yes, the Sweets sell sweets and they love being a little too sweet with me. But they're young and powerful and have the entire world in front of them. While I'm just... well, me. I have no lineage and no prestige behind my name. Well, not yet, at least. I've got big plans to change that.

"You think you can leave without giving us the goods?" Ben sits back in his chair, making the wood creak like it's not meant for that much man.

I smirk, finally giving in to them. By "goods" he means this ridiculous little ritual we've started. Once I told them I see unuseful business ideas everywhere, like it's a compulsion. I thought they would relate. We are in business school, after all. But they didn't and got so much entertainment from hearing my ideas that they now make me tell them the most ridiculous ideas I've had that day.

"Okay, okay," I grin as I stand to put my scarf on. "Today's life-changing business is…" I move my gaze slowly across their faces to build anticipation. "Take a deep breath because your world is about to be rocked. It will affect your family's company too, so take notes…"

Ben tips his huge, muscular frame back in his chair, chuckling under his breath. Deacon takes his baseball hat off and runs his hands through his dark brown hair as he grins at me in anticipation. And Graham has that stoic sparkle in his cool blue eyes that lets me know he's enjoying himself, even if overt displays aren't his thing.

"Don't rush to invest all at the same time, but it's an app that only works on Valentine's Day. People list the chocolates in their box that they don't eat so they can find their perfect chocolate match, a.k.a. the person who eats the ones they don't like and vice versa. Bonus if it's a dating app but I haven't ironed out those details yet."

Graham groans first. "Where do I even begin…"

"Your mind is a terrifying place," Ben says with a laugh.

"Alright, alright." I whip my jacket on. "You can tell me all about how much you love my idea tomorrow. I really have to go."

"Hold on," Graham puts his finger out and reaches into his bag. He pulls out a box wrapped in white paper and an ornate red ribbon embroidered with white flowers. "Just a little something from us. Luckily, your app idea won't be necessary for this since it's full of your favorite dark chocolate salted caramels."

Excitement bursts in me as I take the box from him. Admittedly, way too much excitement over chocolates that are probably more promotional than personal. I'm just really in the mood for chocolate and did not want to buy some for myself on Valentine's Day. And it doesn't hurt that they remembered salted caramels are my favorite.

"You take good care of me. Now my notes tomorrow morning will be extra thorough because I'll be hopped up on chocolate."

"Oh, you're handing out chocolate to the class?" A voice brings our attention to Jessica, a classmate of ours, walking up to the table. I use the moment to tuck their chocolates in my bag and pull on my coat.

"Oh," Graham says awkwardly. "Sorry, we didn't bring any more."

"I'm just teasing," Jessica laughs, flashing her perfect white smile. "I just wanted to ask if you guys have finished the stats assignment, yet? I'm stuck on something."

"Yeah, we did." Graham nods, his golden hair falling over his eyes before he pushes it back. "Which problem?"

"Alright, gotta go," I say again. "Bye, guys. See you, Jessica." I wave at all of them.

"Have fun, Ms. Miller. Oh, and Happy Valentine's Day. We'll miss you." Deacon, always the mischievous brother, says with a wink. It does things to me that I push deep down. Leaving them with Jessica makes way more sense. She's a gorgeous blonde little thing who would match with any of the Sweet brothers much better than me.

Because the biggest difference between us isn't just our stature or status. It's a bit more complicated. Well, it's not complicated at all actually, I just like to pretend that it's complicated. They're almost a decade younger than me. Which means that in addition to being out of my league, we're not even occupying the same planet.

I knew I would be older than a lot of my peers when I decided to get my MBA after years of working on Wall Street. I just didn't anticipate that I would spend so much time with any of them. Or for them to flirt so damn much with me. It's ridiculous. I'm mentally preparing for 40 while 30 is just a fun birthday party for them in their future. That's why despite them being my favorite guys to work with, I know they're just toying with me. They see me as their competent and entertaining little group partner, who they'll forget all about when we graduate.

But tonight I can brush it off easier than other nights. Maybe they're off flirting with Jessica right after they're playing footsy with me under the table. But tonight, I can bet that I'm the one with more exciting plans.

CHAPTER TWO
Emily

I shimmy out of my cab as gracefully as I can manage in a dress and heels. It's a freezing February night, so I pull my fur hood tighter around my face before I whip my phone out to text my best friend, Drea.

> *Emily:* Okay, I just got here. Sharing my location. It's a no phones policy but you'll be hidden smack in the middle of my tits all night under my bra. Congratulations.

> *Drea:* It's kind of nice to know that while I'm reading Mama Llama Red Pajama for the 100th time tonight, there's a version of me that's instead wedged between your tits at a sex club.

I chuckle. Drea and I have been friends since our first day as the only two female interns at Vine Capital, where we both went on to work for years. She went and fell in love though, and now she's making a pretty penny investing their money from the comfort of her Westchester County home while raising her three gorgeous kids. While my only baby is my business idea. But it's a demanding baby of mine and a risky one. I'm using all my life's savings and all my extra time to pursue this dream. Which usually means in the evenings, I'm curled up in front of my laptop late into the night. But *not* tonight.

Tonight, my research has brought me to one of the world's most exclusive sex clubs. The product I want to create revolves around empowering women to communicate openly with their partners about their sexual desires. What better place to learn about that than a sex club full of empowered sex? Even though I've done nothing remotely like this before, it's only in New York City once a year, so I just had to put on my big girl pants and come. It doesn't hurt that it's on Valentine's Day either. I don't usually care about being alone for Valentine's Day, but I can certainly appreciate a holiday-themed activity, which I would argue this is.

I tuck my phone under my jacket and into my bra and straighten my shoulders.

No turning back now.

The event provided me with a code which I now press into a silver metal keypad. When the green light turns on, I push open the giant oak door into a dim hallway. A woman dressed all in black with a plain golden mask covering her eyes ushers me immediately into one of the private curtained spaces lining the entrance. The club is very strict about anonymity and provided me with a scheduled entry time so that the guests don't all pile in at the same time. I imagine that waiting in line would take away some of your will to screw the same strangers later on. I make a mental note to write this observation down later.

She smiles sweetly as she asks for my ID and my phone. I hand over an old decoy phone of mine while my actual phone is lodged safely under the wire of my bra. Once she confirms I'm on the list, she encourages me to choose a mask from the table behind me.

I scan the options. The entry fee for this event was exorbitant but already the quality is evident in the masks. They're all colored gold or black. There is quite a variety, ranging from feminine beaded options that only cover the eyes to a full-head BDSM black latex mask with a zipper on the mouth. I actually let myself consider the full latex mask because not only is it good for anonymity, but as a bonus, I won't have to talk to anyone when I don't want to. I stifle a chuckle. Did I just find out that peace and quiet is my kink? This has already been illuminating. Instead, I choose an option that falls in the middle of the spectrum. It's plain gold and from the nose up it resembles a fox, with pointed ears and everything. It makes sense, as I'm here for my sly reasons.

The woman helps me get it on and then holds up a mirror so I can see myself. Only my bright red lips and my dark brown eyes stare back at me, my usually wild curly hair is pinned back in a loose bun. I'm wearing a silky oxblood-colored dress with thin straps and a draped neckline. It goes perfectly. A nervous smile breaks my composure.

I'm here for practical purposes, but I'm not opposed to taking part if I feel comfortable. My biggest mantra over the last few years has been to honor what I want. Not long after I left my twenties, I realized people stop giving a crap about what a woman is up to in her thirties and beyond. I felt desperate in my twenties to prove to everyone that I was what they wanted me to be. So much so that I barely did anything for myself. Then I finally realized I'm the only person who actually needs to be happy with who I am, so I need to prioritize what works for me. Hence, quitting my job, dumping my asshole boyfriend, and setting myself up to start my own company after I graduate.

The one department I have not progressed in though is getting laid. In some ways, I guess I have, as my sex toy collection has grown extremely thorough. But it turns out that doing what I want has meant staying the hell away from men while I learn what get me going. But now I'm at a sexual standstill and my late-night study sessions with the Sweets have left me surprised by some things I've been craving. So tonight, there is nothing specific I am going to seek, but I'm also not going to deny myself if something catches my interest.

After all, it's simply good research to be open to all possibilities.

CHAPTER THREE
Deacon

What does it say about me that I find a sex club boring? I suppose I shouldn't be surprised. When you grow up with eccentric billionaires for parents, you've pretty much seen it all. The only reason I'm here is because it's our buddy Ted's birthday and he's a horny motherfucker. He's been talking about this event for the past 6 months.

I glance past the blowjobs and pumping asses to read the expressions on Ben and Graham. The same indifference is written all over their body language, and I'm sure their faces, too, if they weren't blocked by these damn masks.

I almost envy the guys we're with who are obviously getting something from being here. They must not have grown up with a father who thought that bonding was bringing his sons to wait around high-end brothels while he and his business buddies disappeared for an hour. Graham, Ben, and I are well-versed in depravity. Graham tried to protect Ben and me as much as he could, but he's only one year older than us. The good thing that came out of such a fucked up childhood is that we're not as defenseless against the shit that drives our friends to become damn hormonal animals. A beautiful naked woman? We've seen a million. A sex club? I'll keep my dick in my pants, thanks though. It's other types of intimacy we're less versed in. That's probably why good banter turns me on more than tits in my face. Blame our father for that fucked up kink of mine.

Graham catches my eye and waves me over to chat with him and Ben.

"I think they're drunk enough that they won't notice if we go to a private room to talk about something other than strangers' asses?" Graham suggests.

"Yeah," Ben nods. "I really don't feel like seeing Ted's cock tonight."

"Let's go before this becomes a dick-measuring contest," I agree. "Don't want to ruin their night by embarrassing them."

We head toward the private lounges, past rows of flat velvet couches where people splay out in all sorts of creative arrangements to get off. Graham leads the way and begins opening doors to see if the rooms are occupied, closing one black door after another with no luck. Finally, he seems to find one and just as he's about to usher us in, I notice a woman bee-lining toward us. I had seen her before a few meters down the hall when she was talking to two other women. In a sex club where everyone is writhing or stripping, casual conversation sticks out like a sore thumb. But another thought went through my mind that I immediately shot down. Something about the way she was hunched over a notebook made me think of Emily Miller. But of course, I'm fucking thinking her. Probably because it's been driving me insane all night thinking that she's out celebrating Valentine's Day with someone. My twisted brain just wants to think she's here instead, ripe for the taking. See? Weird kinks. Of all the women here, only the idea of our goody two-shoes study buddy can get me excited.

As she gets closer, I realize she's coming to talk to us.

We've already had about two dozen propositions from both men and women, so we'll just have to add her to the list of refusals. Even though she is wearing a fucking cool fox mask.

"Um, excuse me. Would you mind if I asked you a few questions?" She says as she gets closer.

"Is that what you get off on?" I ask meeting her brown eyes. That pang of familiarity is more intense now that I'm looking at her straight on.

"Uh, is what?" She bites her lip nervously.

"Asking questions? You get turned on by talking to people?"

A laugh escapes her pretty red lips and my cock twitches before my brain catches up. I know that laugh.

Holy fucking shit. My hunch was right, and it hits me like a damn amphetamine.

Emily Miller.

Our always perfect and composed Ms. Miller…

Is in a damn sex club.

But, no. That can't be right.

She did have to leave our study session early though. A glimmer of relief washes through me, knowing she's not being wined and dined by some Wall Street douchebag.

Why here, though? This doesn't seem like her scene at all.

I don't dare lose my sight on her to glance sideways at the guys but I wonder if they've made the same realization. I trace my eyes down her body and stifle a deep breath seeing her like this. She's all business in school and the few times we've met outside of our projects, she's still dressed like a damn CEO. She never lets her guard down. But this dress shows a side of her I've always had a suspicion was there. The deep red silky fabric dips at her cleavage and shows how her waist arches out to her hips. It's so lusciously feminine in a way she's never wanted to show off at school. I want to touch her. I want to pull her into me and keep her away from the strangers here who couldn't touch her with a fucking fraction of the skill that I would. I know her well at this point after spending two years working alongside her and she deserves only the best.

When our eyes meet, I instantly realize she's nervous. *Fuck.* Either she realizes it's me or she senses some of the filthy thoughts I'm having and thinks I'm a total stranger.

"Ignore him," Ben offers. I can hear the excitement he's trying to hide in his voice. So he knows who our Little Miss Fox is as well? It's no secret between us that we each have this thing for her we can't quite shake. "What can we help you with?" He asks.

"Uh, well, I'm here for research purposes only." She says a bit too defensively and takes her time looking all three of us in the eyes when she says it. I suppress a smirk.

"Oh, it's a research kink then?" I tease her because, well, it's pretty much my hobby at this point and why stop when we're at a sex club? "Well, research away all over us then. What do you want to know?"

"*Not* a kink," she clarifies, and even though she's wearing a mask, I know the exact face she's making under it. A delicious mixture of annoyance and delight that I've caused her to make many times before. "Okay, then, fine. I can make this quick then," she continues nervously. "The first question. On a scale of one to ten, how likely are you to make sure a partner feels safe in this type of environment before, uh, engaging with them?" I look down at her hands and see the tiny pencil and a lone piece of paper in her hand. Of course, that's what she sneaks into a place like this.

"We're not *engaging*," Ben says the word back to her with emphasis, "any women here. We're here for a friend's birthday party."

"Oh, good." she sighs with what I can only recognize as relief. "I mean, not good. But good to know for the research."

She stumbles without her usual finesse and composure and it makes me so fucking happy I want to pull her into a big hug. I love seeing her like this. She's actually nervous for a change. And because of us.

"But hypothetically," Graham adds slowly. "We would make sure that the woman felt extremely safe and ready for *engaging*."

"Good to know," our lovely fox says these words long and slow and everything halts like lightning has struck right in the middle of us. Because there is an edge in her voice. She's picturing herself engaging, a.k.a. fucking, us. And she likes it.

This definitely isn't our steadfastly professional classmate in front of us. This is sex-club-Emily, who wears a mask and lets us under her skin even though we've spent two years trying to do just that with no success.

I watch her suck her bottom lip in and release it, leaving a wet sheen on those beautiful plump lips that I'm more accustomed to watching recite equations in the sterile light of the library. And then I realize... It feels like lightning has struck between us because it fucking has. This is a one-in-a-million chance and I'm not about to miss it.

I reach my hand out and slip my fingers through hers. Her hand is soft and small in mine, but there is no hint of resistance. I lead her to the entrance of the private room we were just about to enter.

"Wh-," she stutters. "Where are we going?"

"The three of us should really answer all your research questions in private," I say, then pause and look back at her so our eyes meet. "*Ms.* Fox."

Her throat bobs. *Busted.*

CHAPTER FOUR
Emily

Sure, when I put this red dress on, I wanted the night to be exciting. But I was thinking that "exciting" would mean some good stories to tell Drea about how I finally learned how an anal plug works from seeing someone else use it. Not being cornered by *them*. The three men that I've always felt embarrassed by how much they affect me, who have always felt like my undoing.

This is bad. This is so bad.

I didn't know it was them when I first approached them. I was so determined to get as much data as I could before I got kicked out or a little too buzzed. But as soon as our eyes met, every part of me realized who I had just cornered.

Maybe I'm misunderstanding, though? Maybe they don't actually know who I am?

No way. Not how Deacon said 'Ms. Fox'. It was the exact same way he calls me 'Ms. Miller'.

Ok, fine. They just want to toy with me, just like all the fake flirting they always do, and I push away. This is no different. I just have to hold it together.

Deacon swings open a black door to a private room and it's

empty. Then he sticks his hand into his pocket and whips out his wallet, using one hand to deftly pull out a couple hundred bills while still gripping me tight with his other hand, like he's afraid I'll disappear if he lets go.

"Make sure no one comes into this room." He addresses the security guard, who is standing a few feet away.

"But-", the security guard protests.

"Not even one person, thanks." Deacon hands him a stack of hundred-dollar bills.

The security guard nods and slips the hundreds into his jacket. "You got it."

I swallow hard, wondering if I should even step through the door.

But Deacon pulls me gently in and I follow like a little puppy. Apparently, something about them being in suits and plain leather masks is causing my brain to malfunction. We pass through the door into the private low-lit room. I slip my hand from his and gravitate toward the back wall to try to gain some composure. I've only had one drink tonight, and it was a super fruity cocktail. So it's not the alcohol that is buzzing throughout my body right now.

I lean back against the wall. The soft velvet fabric lining it glides along the top of my back where my skin is exposed. I take a deep breath and close my eyes. When I open my eyes, the Sweet brothers are lined up in front of me and staring. The three men who have me cornered like prey should scare me. Their broad bodies tower over me and their full attention is intense. But behind those masks are the same eyes that I've stared at across study sessions for almost two years. I know the curves of their broad shoulders and they know my favorite kind of chocolate.

And I also know that I've dreamed about being pinned under any pair of those three shoulders more than any decent person should.

"Any other questions for us, Ms. Fox? This room should give us plenty of privacy." Deacon says as he takes a step closer to me. My pulse quickens as his handsome dark features come more into focus.

A part of me wants to rip my mask off, make a joke, and punch him in the shoulder to bring us back to business as usual. Because, yes, we're friends. We're classmates. But we are not peers, just like we are not, well, potential *partners*. They could hook up with any 20-year-old in this place. Hell, probably any woman in Manhattan. So why are they looking at me like I'm their next meal?

"Well, there is a second question," I finally admit, because it's true and I hate the idea of incomplete data.

"Go ahead," Graham is smiling. Damn, that smile in his mask and suit. It's too delicious.

"On a scale from one to ten, in this particular setting, how much would you value your partner's pleasure in relation to your own?" I ask because this is the question. I've asked many women and men here the exact same question, but the way it comes out of my mouth suddenly sounds like a dare rather than research.

Deacon takes another step closer to me, and I stop breathing. Literally, I am holding my breath. Because I need to use every single one of my senses right now. It's dim as hell in here, there's music playing in the background mixed with an increasing number of moans, and I am not entirely certain that this isn't some depraved sex hallucination due to dangerously low non-self-induced orgasms. Coming to this sex club might have just pushed me over the edge into dry-spell-hallucination syndrome, a new disease for which I am patient zero.

"I value qualitative data more than quantitative data." The words coming out of Deacon's mouth might prove he's still the same graduate student I know so well, but the way he is saying them is dirty as hell. He brushes a strand of hair that fell from my bun behind my ear and I watch him closely. "Rather than us providing a boring number that we could lie about, how about we show you just how much we value *your* pleasure instead?"

"Oh, god," I say out loud before I can stop myself. "Dea-" I start, almost saying his name. "-r." I adjust awkwardly. "Dear. Oh, dear.

I see Deacon's mouth twist in a smile.

"It's just… I'm old enough to be your mother," I blurt out, knowing it's utter nonsense.

Now Ben is laughing. "You're old enough to be our cool aunt at best. You're not even ten years older than us…" He pauses, rubbing his hand on his chin. "I mean, I would guess. Of course, I don't know how old you are." Does this mean he's playing along and pretending we don't know each other? Because, of course, they know my actual age. We've talked about our age difference a million times.

"You think I'm cool enough to be your cool aunt, though?" I fish for more confirmation.

"Well," he debates his answer. "In the *short* time we've known each other, yes." One corner of his lip curves up, a playful smirk forming on his lips.

Yep, he's committing to this game. This steels my nerves. They're going to let me pretend we don't know each other. I take a deep breath. For the first time, I let myself think that maybe I can let my guard down just a little bit. Maybe in this setting, playing this game, I can let myself admit how badly I want them. Maybe I can even get some release from all this damn tension I feel around them. I shudder just at the thought and my lips release a wisp of air.

Deacon is close enough to notice. He brings his hand to my cheek, running his thumb on the corner of my mask. He tilts my gaze up so our eyes meet. Deacon is the most playful man

I know, but right now his eyes are dead serious, even tender.

"Let me kiss you," he says in a deep, hushed tone. "Let me kiss you and if you still think I'm some inexperienced boy who doesn't know how to please you, then I'll stop and walk away and it all stays in this room."

Does he think my hesitance is about him? Of course, it's not. The need to let him know that I've never underestimated him feels suddenly like the most urgent thing in the world. My heart races, a powerful mix of panic and excitement, as I stand up on my toes and guide his head down to mine. He cups the back of my head and flattens his hand against my lower back, pulling me into him. Our lips meet softly. I'm surprised by his tenderness as his plush lips part mine. It's nothing like how I was being kissed in my twenties, usually with drunken sloppiness and a selfish intensity. He continues to kiss me with gentle regard.

Suddenly, a horrible thought hits me. I pull away from him.

"Do you think you need to be gentle with me?"

His eyes have a gleam to them, clearly entertained by my sudden outburst.

He dips low and nips at my ear. Goosebumps branch out down my neck in response. Then he whispers low, "I certainly wasn't planning on it."

CHAPTER FIVE
Emily

With that warning, Deacon's hands wrap around my waist and pull me hard into his muscled body. I gasp at the sensation of our bodies finally touching when I've imagined it a million times. His lips crash into mine and I hungrily match his intensity. A smooth note of whiskey is on his breath and that delicious peppery smell of his is now all I can breathe and all I ever want to breathe again. His tongue finds my bottom lip and then my tongue. Our bodies press against each other and our teeth clash, trying to get more. I'm just about to instinctively rock my hips into him when he steps away.

Panting, he swipes his hand through his dark hair and looks to his side at his brothers as if guilty that he's taken something away from them they want, too. Maybe I should be self-conscious that Ben and Graham saw that, but all I feel is relief to see that they're still here.

"Uh," it's the only thing I can mutter. *Real smooth.* But what the hell am I supposed to say? I'd like to kiss you two now please or otherwise, I'm never going to stop thinking about what it would be like and if this is my only chance, then I'll regret it for the rest of my life if I don't...

The room is silent for a moment. The four of us stare at each other in the all-black room like nocturnal predators, attempting to read body language to see just how much trouble we're all in.

Ben and Graham both take a step at the same time, then look at each other, then at me. I know that it's wrong to want them too after I just kissed their brother. But I do. I want each one of them so badly. So I nod, hoping it's the correct answer to the question that no one is saying out loud.

And it is. They crash towards me. Graham pulls me into him first. It's intoxicating to feel his desperate hands grabbing at my waist. He's usually reserved and in his head, like me. But also, like me, this evening has him coming undone. His kiss is sensual and slow, and I calm my rhythm down to match his. Some of my nervous energy dissipates as I get lost in the heartbeat of the kiss, making me even more aware of the intense ache between my legs that is in overdrive from finally being able to touch them like this.

I gasp into Graham's mouth when I feel a soft tickle of air and lips on my bare shoulder. Ben kisses up my neck to my chin, then grasps my jaw to steal my lips from his brother. My body is on fire and I let out a whimper as Ben pulls me into him and Graham moves behind me to pepper my neck and back with lush kisses.

Ben is the largest of the three and his stature looms over me as I try to tip-toe on my heels to meet him, desperate for more. Our kiss has none of the languid sensuality that Graham's had. Hunger is the only thing vibrating between our bodies. His hands slide down the slick fabric of my dress until he finds my ass, and he takes two big handfuls and steadies me, pulling our waists together. A deep sound comes from his chest when our bodies meet. My hips fight for more contact and I arch into him, feeling delicious steel in his pants, thick and so hard. *Oh god, Ben.* I only think it, even though I want to shout it.

We fight to maintain contact but struggle with the height difference. He takes a breath in frustration, clearly wanting more, just like I do. "Hold on tight," his low voice vibrates into my mouth.

I do as I'm told, wrapping my hands around his neck. His enormous hands trace down my ass onto my thighs and grip me hard. My heart races at the rough contact and I curse myself for wearing stockings, craving his full touch on my skin. He lifts me and presses me against the back wall.

"Oh god," I say as the tight fabric along his hard length presses against my stockings and underwear, lighting up my core with the pressure. I can feel my wetness soaking into my underwear from the contact. I should worry about his dress pants getting stained and never being able to look him in the eye again. That's something that a sane Emily would think about, but all I can think about is getting more friction. Luckily, Ben seems to be on the same page as me as he bucks his hips up and down, grinding his hard cock against me. I sigh into his mouth, a needy beg for more.

"Who the hell wears tights to a sex club?" He growls into my mouth.

"Someone doing *research*." I remind him.

He lets out a low chuckle and I hear Deacon and Graham laugh too and I suddenly feel an overwhelming sense of gratitude for past Emily, who decided to come here. Because this is verging on heaven.

"Right," Ben smiles. I want to rip off his mask to see the full effect of that smile close up, but we're still playing our game. "Your research. Which reminds me."

He places me down gently. His big frame folds before me with lithe ease as he gets on his knees. He bends one of my legs up and slips my black heel off, and then the other. His hands snake up my legs and under my dress until he finds the waistband of my stockings. Our eyes lock as he runs his fingers along the elastic, then digs his hands in and yanks them down. I bring each one of my legs up and watch him as he carefully frees them one at a time. Then he runs his hands up the bare skin of my legs. I savor the feeling of his skin on mine, even if it's not nearly as much as I want it to be. He looks up at me, his hands now on my thighs. I breathe sharply, nerves rattling me. Then with one hand, he grabs the front of my dress and twists it around his hand, lifting it and exposing my red thong for all three of them. I shift back and forth on my feet, nervous about being so exposed. Do they like what they see? Are they going to run away and never look back?

To my relief, he doesn't run away. Instead, he runs his thumb along the ridge in my underwear, and my hips roll, pleading for more pressure.

"Back to the matter." He grins up at me. I know my expression is wild now, begging for more. I'm at his mercy. He turns his head back to Deacon and Graham, who are watching with unflinching intensity. "How do you think we should show her just how much we value her pleasure?"

"I have a few ideas." Graham closes the distance between us and then, to my shock, drops to his knees next to Ben.

Deacon follows next, gracefully moving to the ground.

My chest heaves as I look down at the three of them, on their knees for me.

"Can we taste you now, Ms. Fox?" Deacon asks in a low voice. All I can muster is to close my eyes, lean my head back and nod. Only when I feel my underwear being moved to the side and a delicious warmth spread between my legs, do I summon the bravery to look down.

Three black masks stare up at me as Ben licks long and slow between my legs as if he's savoring the taste. Then he pulls back and tilts my hips to the right, offering me up to Graham.

Graham grabs my hips greedily and pulls me over closer to him. I take a fumbling step and my legs spread wider. He steadies me, pushing my hips against the wall and following with his mouth. He wastes no time devouring me, swirling his tongue and nipping at my clit.

A cry escapes my lips, and my knees falter for a moment before I catch myself. Graham pulls himself away from me and looks up, seeing I'm unsteady. He stands and wraps an arm around my waist and pulls my backside against him.

"We can't have you hurting yourself before your first orgasm," he whispers into my ear and pulls me in tighter. I can only nod in agreement. This whole thing feels like a fever dream and I'm out of my depth. I feel a thick hardness pressing against my lower back and I arch my back against Graham, my body desperate to feel more of him.

Deacon positions himself in front of us, making it clear that now it's his turn with me. Graham holds me tight against him, kissing my neck down to my shoulder as Deacon lifts the silk of my dress and gathers it into a tight fist at my stomach while his other hand explores me. He traces along my slickness until he finds my opening, sliding two fingers in.

He explores me while my body vibrates in anticipation. Then he finds what he's looking for and presses.

A low hum escapes my lips as he presses the perfect spot inside me again. "You like that?" He asks.

"So much." I plead. "Don't stop."

He presses harder inside me and brings his lips to my slit and kisses softly, teasing me. My orgasm looms inside me, threatening to break me open if it's not let out soon.

He sucks my clit into his mouth at the same time he begins pumping his fingers in perfect rhythm. My hips buck with need. He knows he's pushing me as far as I can go.

"I'm so close," I beg. "Please."

"That's so fucking hot," Graham whispers in my ear. "Hearing you beg for what you want."

"Anything for you," Deacon says before pushing his tongue flat against me and lapping me up like he needs my pussy to survive.

Ben stands and brings our lips together in a hungry kiss as my entire body shakes with pleasure. I feel warmth trickling down my legs, but the ecstasy ripping through me is too intense to make sense of it. I let out a cry into Ben's mouth as Deacon keeps working me mercilessly, stretching this crest I'm riding even longer. Every nerve ending is sizzling with sensitivity, but he keeps going.

My body releases again, more intensely than it ever has. Graham is solely responsible for keeping me upright right now, still embracing me against his hard body.

Only when my body stops shaking and is completely spent, do Deacon and Ben pull away. I look down and see Deacon lick his glistening lips, smiling. I don't even understand what just happened. I think I just squirted? That's never happened before. But I've also never felt an orgasm that intensely before.

I look around, dazed, before I notice a weird feeling in my bra.

"Your chest lights up when you come? That's a new one." Ben grins.

In my post-orgasm haze, I finally piece it together that my phone is going off, so I dig it out of my bra. It's Drea. Then I stop, panic ripping through my body. I realize too late that a picture of me and her is her contact photo, so suddenly that's all any of us can look at. Only this big picture of me and Drea is shining at us in the dim room.

Shit. Shit. Shit.

Maybe they've known it's me the whole time, but this is different. Now we can't live in this game we created. We either have to address it now or…

I panic.

"I- I-." I'm stuttering. "I have to go."

If we address it. Everything changes between us. What are we supposed to do? Have a casual conversation about how they just made me come harder than I ever knew I could and I'll see them in class tomorrow? No. My only option is to get the hell away and continue this game. And absolutely never, ever address it.

I grab my heels and run out the door, already feeling incomplete the second the door is in between us.

CHAPTER SIX

Graham

Even the damn passionfruit panna cotta I'm eating is making me horny right now. The fruity zing of flavor takes me back to last night and tasting the delicious citrus on her breath. If I don't fuck Emily Miller soon, my cock might explode. Blood rushes to my waist, a really damn inconvenient time to get a boner. I adjust the napkin on my lap and look up at my father, who is droning on about interest rates.

We're at our biweekly family dinner. Every week would be way too cozy for our family, but every other week is just the right amount of propriety for our old-money parents. I glance at Deacon and Ben sitting across from me. I can tell they're in another world, too. Emily hasn't answered any of our texts. As soon as she ran off, we called her but she ignored the calls. We were on the verge of heading to her apartment and breaking the door down to make sure she got home safely until conveniently our shared document for our Global Strategic Management assignment gave us notifications it was being edited. Instead of responding to us, she went in and started doing edits as if we had just left a damn study session and not an orgy. This was clearly her signaling to us that she's going to pretend nothing happened. The masks gave her just enough protection to deny the night's existence. But the sight of her coming so hard in my arms that her legs dripped with her own juices is so deeply imprinted into my brain that I see it when I close my eyes.

"And finally you boys are almost done slumming it," my dad finally looks at us. This is his way of making conversation.

"If by slumming it you mean going through one of the best MBA programs in the world?" Ben mutters while taking a sip of his whiskey. I'm not sure why Ben even feels the need to defend himself. If I were to compare our father to anything, it would be a blind drunk pig looking for the slop bucket. All he cares about is his next indulgence and he runs everything else over with no awareness to get it. Including his three sons. I don't fight it anymore. I've come to terms with it. He will never change. If anything, it only drives me more to create a fulfilling life because I never want to end up like him.

Before we can get deeper into that topic, a new staff member comes up behind my father. She bends down extra low when she clears his plate and my father ogles her chest, then winks at her.

"Thanks, Alexandra," he says lowly, but still loud enough for the entire table to hear. "And I'll see you later."

He hasn't tried hiding his affairs for at least as long as I've been old enough to understand what an affair is. My mother always just sits there, swirling her drink and zoning out. Maybe they have some arrangement. I don't know, and I don't fucking care.

"Really, dad?" Deacon pipes up as soon as *Alexandra* has left the room. "You can't find a woman not on your payroll to slobber on?"

Our dad shrugs. "Don't pretend you're going to act any different when you're my age."

But among the endless other things our father doesn't know about his sons, this one is the most significant. He doesn't realize that we've worked our whole lives not wanting to be like him. And certainly not like our mother either, who has never stood up for herself or us, terrified of losing her comfortable lifestyle more than her dignity. Thank god my brothers and I have each other in this life because I'm not sure that we would have been able to navigate this hellhole alone.

I'm always relieved to leave our family dinners and move to our favorite neighborhood bar, The Whiskey Drop. We've been coming here since we got fake IDs on Canal Street and ironically, it always feels more like coming home than our childhood home does. We always sit at the bar so we can chat with Meg, our favorite septuagenarian who has known us since we were little shits that couldn't handle our liquor. We're still little shits, but at least we can handle our liquor now.

"So, who's the lucky lady?" Meg asks Deacon, who is looking at his phone.

He looks up at Meg with a sigh. "How can you tell?"

"You've checked that damn phone so much that you didn't even notice my new hair color." Meg cocks an accusatory eyebrow at him. And it's true. Deacon is always the first to lavish Meg with compliments every time we show up and it's some new bright color of the rainbow I've seen on human hair before. But Deacon was probably too busy noticing Emily *not* texting us back to say anything.

"Meg-a-millions," Deacon's voice is thick with praise now. "You're right. I can't believe I missed it. What is that color? Lovely lavender? Luscious lilac?"

I grin, watching Meg eat the attention up.

"Pussycat Plum, actually." She coifs her hair for extra dramatic effect. "Now that that's settled, what's eating you up? Not a great Valentine's Day I take it?"

"Fucking amazing." Ben sounds euphoric and then deflates all within the span of a second. "And then shitty."

"For all three of you?" Meg looks suspiciously at us while she tops off Ben's whiskey. "How does the math on that work?"

"You probably don't want to know, Meg." I offer her an out.

"I've been a bartender in Manhattan for fifty years. You think I haven't seen it all?"

I don't doubt it.

"We're all into the same woman." I shoot back the rest of my whiskey. "We have been for a long time now. And she seems to be into us but won't just…" I stop because I don't know what her damn hold-up is. Sure, logically I can think of a million reasons, but nothing that matters in the scheme of things. But I guess to her, it does.

"Just fucking give in." Deacon finishes my sentence. "She won't just fucking give in."

"You know, I think probably more than half our female regulars started showing up because of you three? Sure, they stay now because of the amazing bartender, but the chance to be with any three of you made some of these women try whiskey for the first time." Meg takes a look around the bar and then back at us. "So, what's wrong with this woman? Is she married or something? That's the trick to finally getting you three, being impossible to have?"

I laugh and shake my head. "She's single. That might be the problem. She's absolutely determined to navigate this world alone."

"Building her own empire," Deacon adds. "She's got big

plans. And I respect it, but I would also pass out with excitement if she ever finally asked us for help. Or at least told us more about her plans than her vague answers about female pleasure while she blushes. News flash, Em, we could help with female pleasure!" Deacon's voice pleads passionately with an imaginary Emily.

Ben slams his drink down on the table after taking a big gulp. "One time," he starts, "her phone died, and she needed to call her friend. The rational thing would have been to ask to use one of our phones. Instead, she disappeared from our study session in a sleet storm to find the nearest phone booth. Phone booths don't even work in New York City anymore. That's how damn stubborn she is about drawing a line with us."

"And the craziest part?" I chime in, laughing. "She fucking found one. The city is supposed to have replaced all of the phone booths, but it wasn't even surprising to us that she, of all people, managed to find the last phone booth in all of Manhattan."

I bring my head up to check if Meg is even still listening when I notice she's doubled over in laughter. Her belly laughs start coming out in high-pitched waves and the other people at the bar turn their heads to see what all the fuss is about. Hell, we're looking at her to see what all the fuss is about.

She stands up straight and wipes a tear from her eye. "Oh," she says, attempting to collect herself. "I'm sorry. I'm just laughing at the universe. Because wow, you managed to find the one person in this whole world who just might be able to handle the three of you." She laughs again to herself. "Most women would crumple up dealing with you three. You're a lot. A lot of looks, a lot of personality, and a lot of power. But this one, bring her round here soon. Because she's a keeper."

She pours whiskey straight into our glasses. "Cheers to her giving you hell. And may you enjoy it."

And we can't argue with that, because yes, she gives us hell. But also hell yes, we enjoy it.

CHAPTER SEVEN
Emily

How long can you ignore your group project members without affecting the quality of the work? Well, it turns out that the answer is longer than I thought. It's been six days of not responding to their texts and calls unless you count the notes in our online shared documents. I'm the editor for our current paper that's due in two days, so I can't really avoid that reality. But we've still been extremely productive without our in-person meetings. Too bad I didn't know this earlier. It would have saved me a lot of trouble.

Of course, it's just like them to continue doing their work perfectly despite all the bat-shit craziness going on. I could almost resent them for it if it didn't mean getting perfect grades.

I finish editing a paragraph that Graham added about the methodology we used for our conclusions and it's immaculate. I add a note.

Emily Miller: *Great addition. No notes except to add a reference to this in the introduction.*

* * *

I've also managed to keep up with my work as if last week never happened. Because it essentially didn't. We were wearing masks. We have plausible deniability here. So that means I am going to continue to act like it never happened even if my insides are all gooey and confused. I just have to ignore their texts forever, which allude to that night, and continue dodging them after class. I've done harder things.

A chime goes off on my computer. A new comment from Deacon Sweet was added.

Deacon Sweet: *Get your ass to the library or we're sending this paper in before your final revisions.*

I swear. He's got to be bluffing. They care about their grades and reputation just as much as I do. Every professor in our program has incredible connections and sway in the industry. One sloppy paper could mean losing all of that access. I write back in a panic.

Emily Miller: *You wouldn't dare.*

Graham Sweet: *You have one hour.*

Oh god. That last comment is from Graham. Graham is just as much of a perfectionist as I am. If he's willing to do this, then they're serious.

I rush to the bathroom to throw water on my face and take a look at myself in the mirror. Mostly, my reluctance to see them is delaying facing what happened between us for as long as possible until we can all just forget it. Even though that seems unlikely to happen for me. It's been almost a week and I can still barely control myself when I think about that night. Blood rushes to my cheek and a delicious warmth burrows under my skin. My body takes over and begs for more of whatever the hell it had that night. So what will happen when I actually see them? I like to think I'm a woman who has my shit together, but they make me feel like a giddy schoolgirl.

But there's another aspect, too. And I hate it. But they make me feel self-conscious. My eyes have crow's feet where theirs bounce back. My body and skin have changed even since the last time I've been with a man before them. I've worked hard on self-acceptance because let's be real, hating on myself is a waste of time that I simply don't have. But they're so damn young and beautiful that, of course, I'm thinking about it. We were wearing masks, and the lighting was dim that night. What would happen if I give myself to them and they decide they don't want it? How could I recover? I'm already afraid of losing them as my friends, but what if I lose my confidence too?

I've worked so hard to empower myself. I need my next steps after grad school to succeed. I don't have any Plan B, I'm putting everything into starting my business. And I need to be in the right head space for it. Raising capital for a start-up is hard enough for a woman as it is, without being swept up in this chaos. I'm already flustered and distracted from just that one night. What would happen if I gave them more? Or worse, they stop wanting more?

The answer is easy. We will never need to know because we won't find out. Whatever happened that night will forever be locked away in that club. All I have to do when I see them is keep my demeanor firm and not turn as deep red as the silk dress that's hanging in my closet because I can't bring myself to wash their scent off of it.

I rush into the library and scan for them in our usual spot, but they're nowhere to be found. I pace around, looking for them, my heart racing. It's been 40 minutes since they sent that message. I couldn't resist still trying to look my best because, well, I have a pulse.

I spot a tall stature filling one of the private study rooms and already I can feel myself blushing. The last time I saw that silhouette it was...

Focus.

I dart into the room.

"I'm here." I pant. "Don't you dare send that paper!" I sit myself down in an empty chair and shuffle in my bag for my laptop and open it up.

Deacon's troublemaking smile greets me. "Hello, Ms. Miller. We've missed you." He walks over to the table and shuts my laptop closed. "Care to share with us where you've been?"

Crap.

I can't bring myself to look him in the eye for too long. Not without melting into a puddle. Ben closes the door behind me and I wonder why the hell they had to choose a private study room when there were plenty of tables in the main room available. This room is small and filled with the smell of them that immediately takes me back to that night. Those delicious spicy undertones are everywhere. *Fine.* I'll just breathe through my mouth then. I won't be poisoned by their addictive pheromones today.

"I've been really busy." My voice sounds nasally, without a functioning nose.

"Oh? With what?" Ben pries.

"My, uh," I pause, my brain is short-circuiting as their large frames surround the table. "My, uh... uncle is in town."

"Your 'uh, uncle', huh?" Graham cocks an eyebrow.

"Yup, sorry if I've been bad at responding. He's never been

to New York City, so I've been so busy showing him everything." I double down, ignoring his obvious skepticism. I train my eyes on the table instead of Graham because he's wearing his dress shirt unbuttoned at the top and his sleeves are rolled up. That look on him has always done intense things to me, but right now it's downright unfair.

"Oh, that's nice of you." I chance to look up at Deacon to see what he's playing at. He has that gleam in his eye that tells me to brace myself. "Well, you should bring your 'uh, uncle' to our box for the Knicks game tonight. We'd love to meet him."

"Oh," I frown. "No. Thank you, though."

"What's the problem?" Deacon's eyebrows knit with a bit too exaggerated concern. Why won't they just politely let me get away with this lie? Just give it to me?

"Well, no need to bore you guys with my uncle. You just have fun without us."

"I don't understand," Deacon continues. "You'll let us taste your pussy but won't introduce us to your uncle?"

I practically choke on my own gasp. I take a huge breath of air that I haven't been able to do without breathing through my nose. I glance around me, making sure no one is within earshot.

"Don't worry about anyone else." Ben stands up and closes the heavy curtains that line the glass wall of our study room. He paces back to me and gets right into my space. His muscled thighs in his dress pants and thick cognac leather belt are suddenly all I can look at. I'd take this view over anything else. I've been dreaming of waking up in a Paris apartment overlooking the Eiffel Tower, but suddenly that doesn't seem like a worthy goal because where do Ben's thighs fit in? Which is exactly why I need to stop this madness. I tear my eyes away and look back down at the table. But Ben has other plans. He places his thumb under my chin and gently angles my face up to look at him. His dark brown eyes always look kind, but right now they look different. They look at me like they want to eat me whole.

"That night at the club happened." He says firmly. I feel myself blush immediately. "And it was amazing. And we know there's no uncle in town. So now tell us the real reason you're ignoring us."

I hate the fuzzy blanket that is wrapping around my brain currently and cutting off all the blood flow that I need for rational thought. Ben's light touch is enough to make my resolve weak. And hearing him call the night amazing is even more debilitating.

"I thought there was an unspoken agreement that it was just a one-time thing that would never be mentioned again. We got carried away." I say calmly, with all the strength I have left to muster.

"What was it about that night that made you think we wouldn't bring it up again?" Graham gets closer to me now, too. I swallow hard, readying myself for his interrogation. "Was it when we each took turns tasting you for the first time? Or when I held you in my arms as your whole body trembled, coming over and over again?"

A small sigh unintentionally escapes my lips. I glance at the door. Maybe I should just run out now. Because what the hell do I say to that? I notice Graham's entire body language shift as if he's ready to catch me, his runaway fox, if I dare move toward that door.

"I don't understand," I say softly in resignation. "Why would one of you want me? Let alone all three? You could have anyone you want. And why risk making this good thing we have so messy?"

"We want you only," Deacon says without missing a beat as if he's been ready for this question. He moves toward me to get in alignment with his brothers. Suddenly, our formation is dangerously close to exactly how it was that infamous night. Right before everything went down. "Why is that so hard for you to believe? You're confident and you dominate in every other facet of your life. You're a force, Emily. You get what you want. So why can't you believe that you deserve what you want when it comes to us? Because I think you do want us."

I swallow. Are they what I want? Is it even possible to want all three of them? I shake the thought away.

"I'm ten years older than you." I fight back. "You guys probably don't even understand why some contact information has a space to fill in a home phone number. You see, when I was growing up, we still had phones that-"

"Older men are in happy relationships with younger women all the time." Graham interrupts me. "They seem to survive the decade-long gap in home phone technology." His eyes are smirking, but he just hit on the root of my angst without knowing it. My heart races for a very different reason. This time it's a symptom of my brain kicking back into action.

Because he's exactly right. Older men go for younger women all the time. Because that's the reality we live in. Age *does* matter. At least for half of the population. Women need to be less for men. Less in age, less in demands, less in physical stature, and less eager to conquer the damn world like I want to. Maybe I'm novel to them right now, someone different from who they normally go for. But I don't have time to be a tourist attraction they stop at on their way to pretty young wives. No matter how much pleasure I might be denying myself, nothing is worth giving up my focus.

"I need to go," I shake my head. "I'm sorry. I just can't."

And with that, my head finally makes a good decision and forces my feet to do what they should have done last week. Walk the hell away before it's too late.

CHAPTER EIGHT

Ben

"Just sex then," Graham says firmly just as Emily's hand grips the door handle. I look at Graham with a confused expression, but he doesn't take his eyes off of Emily. "Your plan is to be the next big thing in the female pleasure industry. You want to tell people how to have sex, so look me in the eye and tell me you've ever come as hard as you did with us."

She takes her hand off the door handle and my shoulders fall in relief. If she walked out that door right now, I'm not sure how we would have gotten her back.

"Learn with us. Experiment with us. Hell, *use* us." Graham finishes his plea and Emily lets out a long, defeated sigh. He's offering her any version of this that she feels comfortable with. Whatever this is between us is unavoidable. If she has to signal to that big brain of hers that this is just about her business, then hell, we'll let her. Graham is always a genius, but this is the first time that it might actually pay off with something useful.

"I've never fully explained my business to you, though." She turns around with a skeptical look. "Do you even understand what you would be getting into?"

Graham breathes deep in relief. Because I know what he knows, too. That there isn't a thing on this planet that we would say no to. Is her business plan to open a dildo shop where she exclusively molds the Sweet brothers' dicks? Sure no problem. A live-stream sex show? We'll get naked right now.

"Tell us, Foxy," Deacon is smiling now. I can tell the man is practically pissing himself with excitement. He knows we're in, too.

Emily blushes and I can't tell if it's from her new nickname or the business plan she's about to finally explain to us after our two years of asking and only getting dodgy answers.

"Well, I have a lot of plans, but I'm going to start with one very simple idea." Emily starts, taking turns to look at us all in the eyes.

We're waiting with baited fucking breath, but I try to convey encouragement and patience in the limited eye contact she allows.

She breathes in deep. "The core idea is communicating about sex. Most men don't even know where the clit is and in our society, women can be afraid to ask for what they want. So I would start with a very simple app that has games built in for couples to use. Some ideas would include quizzes on preferences and having to guess what your partner answers, scientific facts about pleasure and how it can vary from person to person, and even clit stimulation simulation which is pretty catchy and a goldmine for marketing." She smiles. I can hear her excitement clinging to every word. "It's not about bringing a phone into bed, but it's a starting point to talk about things that might be uncomfortable for some people."

"I think it's a great idea. And so much potential to branch out to different products." I nod. And I mean it. The women

I've been with have been terrified to ask for what they want. In fact, Emily was the first person I'd ever been with that even dared ask for more. And it was fucking hot.

She inhales and then exhales. "Thanks, Ben. But Graham is right about something. I haven't really tested any of my ideas. That night with you guys was the end of the longest dry streak of my life." She's talking now like the Emily we know. Excited about working things out with us, her best guys "It's kind of ironic working on a sex app," she continues. "Because I've essentially sworn off men. At this point, I was debating just pivoting to a rating website for dildos because that's become my new expertise."

I inwardly groan in frustration, imagining her shoving a big dildo into herself. There have been so many nights that we've said goodbye at the end of working together where all I wanted to do was pull her in for a kiss, grab her by the waist, and take her against a library bookshelf. My body has been screaming for her. I wonder how much her body has been screaming back and how many times she thought about us when she touched herself over the past two years.

"Let's do it," my voice sounds lower and menacing than I mean it to. "Communicate what you want to us and we'll do it. It will be your first test of concept, but also this way we won't do anything you're not comfortable with."

Emily taps her foot nervously, considering. I stop myself from getting on my damn knees and begging.

"Okay, but it only works if we establish an end date. I need to start raising capital in April and I need full concentration when I start." She looks at us expectingly.

I hate the idea of an end date. It feels so unnatural.

I look to Deacon and Graham. We each know it's the only way we're winning this battle.

"Fine, if that's really what you want. This ends at the end of March, then." I concede.

"It is what I want." She nods. "All in agreement?"

We nod, clearly not loving the idea of it ending, but fucking ecstatic about the rest.

"And when would we start?" She asks. The fear I sensed earlier is gone and replaced with that same determination she has when working on a particularly difficult project.

I don't want her to slip out of our hands. If she walks out that door, she might put the Great Wall of Emily back up again.

"It's only right that we have you for the first time right here in the study room, you little nerd." Deacon smiles wickedly. I look up to see how Emily reacts and I'm relieved to see that it's echoed with excitement in her eyes.

"Oh god," she says as a flush crawls from her cheeks down her chest between the opening of her button-up shirt. Her whole body is already on fire and we've barely gotten started. She breathes out as if she's climbing a mountain and nervously shakes her hands outward to collect herself. "Okay, I've got to get it together. If I'm going to be starting an entire business about sex, then I should be able to do the bare minimum and talk to you guys about the, ugh, possibility."

"I'd say it's more of a sure thing." Deacon winks at her.

She takes another deep breath. I love how much we're working her up without laying a hand on her. "Okay, well, for research purposes, maybe we could exchange things we might be into, want to try, or want to stay away from."

"Ugh, well," Deacon starts. "We've made it clear we want to have sex with you, right? In case we haven't, I'd really fucking like to put my penis in your vagina."

This gets an exasperated laugh from Emily. "Yeah, okay, good starting point. I should be more specific, though." She looks up at the ceiling, her thinking face. "Well, for example, the other night when I was with you, my body did things I didn't even know it could do."

"You came so hard that you squirted and made me practically die right then and there from being so fucking turned on." Graham fills in helpfully.

"Ugh, yeah that." She looks everywhere in the room but at him. "I've never done that before. Is that a thing that you like to make women do? Are you into that?" She's addressing Deacon now, who was the one who made it happen. I brush away the ping of jealousy I have that he made her body do that before I did. Because I sure as hell plan to do the same.

Deacon shrugs. "I was afraid it would be the only chance I ever got to make you come, so I put my heart and soul into it, to make sure you come back to me begging for more." He cocks his eyebrow. "Instead, a damn paper got you back here."

Emily smiles. I'm glad she's relaxing a little.

"So you're asking us if we have any kinks?" I offer. It's not that I don't respect the process, I do. But my cock is also fucking starving for her. My kink *is* her. And I don't know how to explain that without making her run away.

"That," she nods. "Or something specific you'd like to try. Something that maybe you might enjoy that you've never tried."

The only thing I can think of right now that I've never tried is burying my cock deep into her pussy and hearing her moan my name. But I stay quiet. In fact, for a record amount of time, all three of us aren't saying anything.

"Okay," she nods. "This is why I'm testing this approach out. It clearly needs tweaking."

She taps her thumb against her thigh, a tic of hers that I've seen a million times when she's trying to solve a problem. She opens her mouth to speak, but then closes it again.

"Go ahead," I encourage her. "Nothing you could say would scare us off right now."

"I can start with something I'd like to try this session, and then we can see how it works."

Session. How very romantic. But even the sterile white surfaces of the study room and her straightforward approach can't stop the pure fucking need for her thrumming in the veins of my cock. She could ask for any of the dirtiest and most depraved cravings, and I'd give them to her. Hell, I'm already willing to fuck her in front of my brothers.

"Give us your first wildest fantasy, Foxy. We're the men to get it done."

"I want talk. Dirty talk." She blurts out before she can let her brain stop her.

"Perfect," I say, picking up the torch she just passed us. I'm so fucking ready to get this show on the road. "Now quiet that big, gorgeous brain of yours enough to let your pretty pink pussy get what it wants."

Her eyes go big. Because I know this woman. She is a perfectionist in everything she does. She practically squeals in excitement when she gets her never-ending supply of perfect grades back. She doesn't just want dirty talk; she wants praise. And I have so much fucking praise ready for her.

CHAPTER NINE

Ben

I box her in against the door, reminding her that leaving is off-limits until we do what we damn well should have done a long time ago. I waste no time bringing my mouth to hers and kissing the hell out of her. There's no reserve left in me.

I breathe her in as I kiss her with pure hunger. Our tongues lick and plead for more. She pulls my waist in and I groan.

"You feel how bad I fucking want you?" I push my rock-hard cock against her stomach. "All I can think about is feeling you dripping all over me while I fuck you like you've never been fucked."

A delicious hot gust of breath leaves her mouth. She *does* like the dirty talk. But what she doesn't know is it's not just dirty talk, it's a damn fortune telling.

"Wait," she pulls back. Panic sets in me. Is she trying to leave again?

She slips away from the door and attempts to swivel me but I'm still stuck in place wondering why the fuck I'm not dry humping her right now.

"I want to return the favor," she explains, and I finally let her guide me and push me against the door. "To all three of you." She motions for Deacon and Graham to come over closer.

We all are clearly unsure what she means, but listen anyway, our boners leading the way and doing whatever the hell she says.

Then I understand what she means as she starts unbuckling my pants and gets on her damn knees.

"Emily, you don't owe us anything." Graham offers. *Right.* I probably should have said that when she started unbuckling my pants.

"It's what I want," she says. "Will you let me?"

"Fuck yes," I offer a little too quickly.

She looks up at me with a grin, but I catch something else. She's nervous. I stroke a loose curl behind her ear. "But we can take it slow, too."

"Ben, don't make me beg you to suck your dick," she finishes unbuttoning my pants.

"I don't know," I grin. "That sounds kind of nice, too." But I help her move my pants down and step the fuck out of them quicker than anything I've ever done.

"Just get your dick out and put it in my mouth before I say something I'll regret," she runs her hands along the tight black fabric covering my length. I laugh and shudder at the same time and damn, that's a nice combination of sensations I didn't even know I liked.

I grab her hand, place it on my stomach, and push it under the elastic waistband until it finds my raging erection. She grips her soft fingers around me and immediately my dick pulses in her hand. She pulls it out of the tight constraint of my boxers.

"Woah, Ben," she cocks an eyebrow at me. "You've got a beautiful dick."

"Thanks. I've been waiting for you to notice," I tease her.

She laughs. Then turns to Deacon and Graham. They help

her unbutton their pants and she pulls their hard-ons out of their boxer briefs, too. I see restraint barely holding them together as she smiles up at them the same way she did to me.

"It's clearly the genes," she says, but this time swallows hard. With our three cocks heavy and ready for her, I wonder if she's feeling like she's bitten off a little more than she can chew. I know she's mirroring the way we got on our knees for her on Valentine's Day at the club, but it's a little different with her having to handle all three of us. Although she's always been a damn hard worker.

I'm about to get down on my knees and meet her on the floor until I see something else in her eyes when she turns back to me. She licks her lips and that gorgeous face is excited. She loves seeing all three of our cocks exposed and rock-hard for only her. And I certainly fucking like seeing her want us. I almost lose it at this sight alone.

She looks up at me. "Ready?"

"So fucking ready, Em." My voice feels unfamiliar in my throat, so taken over by lust for what she's about to do. Her eyes smile as she looks up at me and grabs my shaft, bringing the tip to her lips. I sharply inhale as she takes little licks around my tip, taste-testing me. Then she slowly guides me into her mouth, swirling her tongue around my girth until she can't anymore. I watch as her lips stretch to accommodate me. She moves back and forth slightly, making sure I'm slick. It can't be easy. My cock takes up her whole fucking mouth. But she doesn't stop. She keeps going and going, sliding me down the back of her throat until she gags and looks up at me, holding me there as I'm as deep in her throat as physically possible.

Fuck.

I spread my fingers through her hair and admire her big brown eyes looking up at me. "You look so damn beautiful with my cock filling your mouth." I try to keep my composure as I grit out the words. She bobs her head, fucking me with the back of her throat, and I close my fist around her hair in pleasure. I don't blink because I don't want to miss a damn second of this. She gags herself with me, and somehow pushes me even deeper than I knew a woman could. But this is Emily Miller sucking my cock. She does everything with her full capacity, and it turns out this is no different.

I moan as I feel her throat constricting and releasing around the sensitive head of my dick.

"Fuck, Emily." I groan. "I don't want to come yet, but you're bringing me goddamn close."

She slides off me and takes a deep inhale, catching her breath.

She wraps her hand around me and then looks up at Graham. She takes a different approach with him, licking his shaft up and down, making it shine with her saliva before she puts him in her mouth and bobs and licks his tip while she fists his base. Fuck, she's got multiple ways of sucking cock and she's sampling each of us with them. I want to try the entire damn menu.

By the time she moves to Deacon, my brain is going into overdrive. It's intimate seeing their moments together and how much they both love this just as much as I do. But then I look at Emily, enjoying it too. Seeing her so hungry for us is the sexiest thing I've ever witnessed. I've always known she likes us. You don't spend as much time together with people you don't like. But she *wants* us. Just as badly as we've wanted her since the moment we first sat across from her.

"Come here," I grab her shoulders after she takes a breath from having Deacon's cock in her mouth. I lead her to the table. I want to throw everything off the table like a goddamn caveman, but Emily would kill me if I did that to her laptop and I can't die before I bury myself inside her. So instead, I stack her things in a neat pile on a chair.

She looks at me, confused, so I swipe her up under her legs and lay her down on the table. "I don't want to wait while you finish off my brothers' cocks. I need you right fucking now. We're multitasking. I know you're great at it." She laughs nervously but nods her approval and waves Deacon and Graham over.

"Now let's get these fucking pants off," I groan as I fidget with the clasp of her black dress pants. Of course, she's dressed like she's attending a board meeting, and it's still sexy as hell.

"And this shirt needs to get the fuck off," Deacon reads my mind while he works on the tiny little buttons of her white silk shirt.

I pull down her pants and throw off her heels with desperate speed as Deacon and Graham slip her shirt off.

There she is. Our Emily. Finally, spread out in her little black panties and bra for us. I'm suddenly so grateful for the bright lights of the library because I'm going to commit every inch of her to memory. I trace my eyes along the curve of hips to her waist and then up to admire her heavy tits that I've imagined a million times under those dress shirts she wears. But her hands are cupping her chest as if she's trying to hide them. No, fuck that.

I wrap my fingers around her wrists and move her hands to Graham and Deacon's exposed cocks bobbing over her. She grabs onto them.

"Does that feel like two men who want you to cover your sexy tits?" I ask. She eyes me wildly in surprise. I guess she's shocked I picked up on what she was doing. Of course, I picked up on it. She's the only thing I'm laser-focused on right now.

I rub my thumb along the lace of her bra and over her nipple and then trace along her stomach until I reach the edge of her underwear.

"Can I?" I practically beg.

"Yes," she nods enthusiastically, and Deacon bends down to kiss her. I watch the two of them kiss as I slide my ring finger down her panties. I trace along her warmth until I find her opening and push my finger into her. She is so goddamn wet for us. I swear under my breath, forcing myself not to plunge my cock into her this second.

She gets up on her elbows, chasing after her kiss with Deacon, and I notice her bring her hand down, trying to hide her stomach this time. Now Graham and Deacon notice it.

"Foxy, you've got three men surrounding you hard as fuck. There simply isn't time for you to be self-conscious. You're fucking perfect and you've got a lot of orgasms to have, and frankly, so do we."

"I know," she groans in frustration. "I just haven't been with anyone in a long time. I mean, besides the other night with you guys, if that counts."

"Oh, it definitely counts," Graham walks over to her side and runs his hand along her clavicle and then down to her breasts and palms them out of her bra. He bends over, taking her pink nipple in his mouth, then pulls away an inch. "You're so beautiful," he whispers. "I would just jack off right here to this sight and be happy."

Emily visibly relaxes and smiles. "I wouldn't," she looks up at him. "I've got other plans for you." She reaches out to his cock and begins stroking him and beckoning him closer until she has him in her mouth. I stroke her clit up and down slowly as she works Graham's cock back and forth with her mouth. She pulls away and bends her head back to find Deacon, and guides him down her throat. I see her pale throat bobbing as she works him with pure commitment. I wasn't sure how I would feel seeing her like this with them, but it's so fucking hot to see how badly she wants us all. I rub her clit harder and her hips arch and drop in need.

She pulls away from Deacon and looks at me, impatience written all over her face.

"Tell me you want me inside you," I say slowly as I flick her clit back and forth.

"Ben, would you please finally just get the hell inside me?"

I grin. "I thought you'd never fucking ask." I run over to my pants on the floor and pull out the condom I packed earlier when I was feeling hopeful we'd see her. I tear the wrapper open with my teeth and roll the latex over my cock impatiently.

I grip her hips hard and admire her soaking wet pussy. I drag my cock along her slit. She writhes with impatience until I push into her, pinning her to the table. I rock once, coating my tip with her juices, and then I push my entire length in, inch by inch until she's full to the hilt with me. She braces herself, splaying her fingers on the table.

"Holy shit," she gasps. I take long and steady pumps in and out, loving how well she takes me, clenching around me as if her body has been waiting for this. Fuck knows mine has.

"Your body is fucking meant to take my cock," I tell her and she moans in response. I grip her hips tighter, barely holding onto my composure. For the first time, I wonder how soundproof this room is, because I need to hear her screaming for more.

I look up at Deacon and Graham, and a moment flashes between us. This is finally fucking happening, their expressions say.

I pull out suddenly and love seeing Emily's face turn desperate, searching for why I stopped.

I bend down and kiss her stomach before backing away. "Sorry, Em. I'd be the worst brother in the world if I didn't let them experience how good you feel."

CHAPTER TEN
Emily

I wrap my hands around Graham's neck as he pulls me up on the table and presses me into his chest. I feel his thick cock pressed in between our stomachs and my heart flutters that he's going to be inside me soon, too. He flips us so that he's sitting on the table and I am straddling him. Once we're settled, he pulls me in for a deep kiss.

"Do you know how long I've waited for this?" He says into my lips and then nips at my bottom lip.

I shake my head no. Because my brain is starting to short-circuit and I don't have any brain power left in me to even try to guess.

"From the very first day I met you," he grabs my ass and pulls me tight against his erection. I grind against him, loving how the smooth velvet skin feels against my clit. His words bloom in my chest. I thought they were teasing me when they were such flirts. But have they really wanted me for that long? Do they feel as addicted to me as I do to them?

Ben hands Graham a condom, and he breaks our bodies apart to put it on. A part of me wants to beg him to not use one, but I fight it because I know that would be insane. I would use protection without a second thought with any man, but now suddenly I'm ready to go without with three men? What the hell has gotten into me?

The Sweet brothers. That's what. They are the most intoxicating men I've ever come across.

"I'm going to sit you right on top of my cock," Graham says gruffly in my ear while biting at my lobe. He traces kisses down my neck. "And then I'm going to let Deacon have his turn with you, too."

I swallow hard. "What do you mean?"

I feel light, warm kisses down my back.

"We're going to take turns with you, Foxy," Deacon's voice purrs into my ear. "You want that?"

Damn.

Yes, I want that.

I didn't even know that was a thing I wanted one second ago, but now my core throbs for it. Just the thought has me at my edge.

I whisper a breathless agreement and my voice sounds high-pitched and out of control.

Deacon laughs a low, seductive laugh of approval. And then Graham does as he promised and lifts my hips up, aligning his tip at my entrance, and pulls me down back on top of him. I whimper and grab tight onto his shoulders. I close my eyes as he fills me up and our bodies find their rhythm. I'm already sore from Ben, and Graham's cock stretches me even more in this position. But it's a delicious soreness because it comes with being so full of him that every single nerve is alive and on fire.

I open my eyes to see Ben's eyes burning into mine, standing against the wall and stroking himself. I love seeing the way he handles his massive erection and I take note of the way he rubs his tip, eager to try it myself on him.

Suddenly, I feel another pair of hands on my ass, spreading

me open and guiding me up and down on Graham. I look back to see Deacon greedily eyeing my body.

"You've been hiding an ass like this from us, Foxy? It feels so fucking good in my palms."

A filthy desire for him to fuck my ass shivers through my body.

"Mm," Graham moans. "She likes that." He says as he drives harder into me.

"Fuck," Deacon's eyes meet mine. "I need to be inside you. Now."

I can only nod frantically in approval.

Deacon lifts my thighs up off of Graham and Graham bends back on the table, holding me tight and bringing me with him. Deacon pushes my thighs back down, locking Graham's wet cock between our stomachs. I'm straddling Graham, but spread wide open for Deacon.

Deacon plunges into me while Graham tips my face up to his to kiss me. Deacon thrusts into me harder than his brothers and I bite down on Graham's lip in ecstasy.

I can't control myself any longer. Being pressed in between them like this while Deacon slams into me is my undoing.

I cry out and just when I think I can't feel any more pleasure, Graham starts rocking his hips so the pressure of his cock is sliding along my clit. A guttural yell comes from my mouth, and my thighs shake uncontrollably. I hear the sounds of my release escaping as Deacon continues to slam into me.

"Fuck, you're coming so hard, Emily." He says, out of breath. "I can't hold it any longer."

Deacon thrusts into me, his cock bucking inside me, and my orgasm rips through me again.

Graham grips my head from either side and lifts it, watching my face closely as I orgasm.

"Damn it, Emily. You look so fucking pretty when you come." He says as he rocks his cock against my clit and stomach in a steady motion. My eyes flutter open and shut, trying to gain any control, but ecstacy still has a full grip on my body. I see Graham's face twist and a groan escape his lips, then he pulls me in tight to him as his body trembles below mine. I think about yelling for him to get inside me, but he's already coming and I'm too lost in my own passion. I collapse into his chest, kissing the skin of his tight, firm pec.

I see Ben charging towards us out of the corner of my eye. Deacon pulls himself out of me.

"Keep coming for me, baby," Ben commands. "I need to feel that pussy grip mine as I come in you."

My heart starts racing again and I nod into Graham's chest. I want that too. So badly. My greediness surprises me, but that thought quickly vanishes as Ben thrusts into me. I'm already so sensitive that every thrust is like an explosion through my body, a twinge of pain but a tidal wave of pleasure.

I dig my nails into Graham's muscled arms as Ben pounds into me harder.

"You're taking us so good, baby," Graham whispers in my ear, and I cry out in response.

"Fuck, Emily," Ben shouts in a voice that, in all my stupor, I can still recognize is probably too loud for where we are.

He slams one last time into me, and I feel his huge cock throb with his orgasm. The extra pressure carries me over an edge I didn't even know I had and I cry in pleasure into Graham's chest, as my core clenches Ben in turn.

After a moment, I release a long, satisfied sigh. And as my body starts to relax, my mind starts to turn on again.

For a long while, only the sounds of our panting fill the room.

"What *was* that?" I finally whisper. I'm not sure if I'm asking them, or myself. Or even what I'm asking at all. I just didn't even know my body could do all that. I didn't even know having all three of them was an option. And I definitely didn't know that the three of us, usually perfectly professional, could devolve into fucking like damn animals in the library, of all places.

"*That* was just the beginning." Ben squeezes my ass as he pulls out of me.

An excited smile dances at the corner of my lips. The thought that we could do this again is just...

Knock. Knock.

I don't get to finish that thought.

"Crap!" I hiss at them, scurrying off of Graham. I frantically try to find my clothes while the guys do the same.

"One second," Deacon says as he buttons up his shirt. He's the first to be ready, so he cracks open the door.

"Yep?" He says to whoever is on the other side.

"Uh, hi." I hear a high-pitched feminine voice. "I was just waiting for you guys to be done with your study session because I had a couple of questions for you. But then it sounded like you guys were fighting so I waited..." She pauses. I recognize that voice. It's Jessica. The woman I've always imagined one of them might pursue. My heart sinks a little at the reminder, but hey, at least it's not the cops. "Um, yeah." She continues when Deacon says nothing. "But it sounded quieter so I just knocked."

"What's your question, Jessica?" Deacon says with a clip of impatience. "We're just finishing an intense study session and I'd like to get back to it."

"Oh, well. It wasn't just one question. I wanted to pick your guys' brains about last week's class."

Pick their brains. Mm hm. That's one way to try to say it.

"Sorry, we're pretty busy with our own stuff. Do you know who takes really good notes? Michael. I bet he'd love to help you."

"Michael Steed?" She says with disgust. Michael Steed is

one of the smartest guys in our class, not sure why she says his name with such resentment. Probably because he's not as drop-dead gorgeous as the Sweet brothers, but that also covers about everyone else on the entire planet.

"Yep, Emily was just making a truly amazing point. So if you don't mind, I'm going to get back to her." He nods at her as she makes little sounds of objection, but he closes the door.

"She thought we were fighting," he grins and pulls me into a hug. I savor the affection, even though I know I shouldn't. "I should have told her, yes, we were. Fighting over your pussy."

"Now just try not to walk out of here with a limp, and I think we'll get away with this one." Ben takes my hand and kisses it.

"Next time, we're doing this at our apartment." Graham kisses the top of my head.

And against my better judgment, I realize those might be the two most delicious words I've ever heard. *Next time.*

"Next time." I agree.

CHAPTER ELEVEN
Emily

I take a little too long savoring the taste of the chocolate cake, licking it slowly and luxuriously from the spoon and closing my eyes to savor the flavor. When I open my eyes, Drea is staring at me with open mouth fascination. I burst out laughing when I realize how ridiculous I look.

"Damn, girl. It's like you've been locked in a cave and are only just now discovering sweetness." She takes a sip from her wine, eyeing me.

Mmm. Sweetness. Just the word gets my heart racing. The Sweet brothers.

"Keep it in your pants over there," Drea grins. "But seriously, I'm happy for you. I'm not sure I've ever seen you this relaxed."

I explained everything to Drea over a rare night out for dinner in the city with her. She's likely the only person in the world I would confide in about all this. When you go through your sloppy twenties together, there's no sense in hiding anything for the rest of your lives.

"I *am* relaxed." I nod. "I'm present in my body if that makes sense? But also a part of me is kind of mad. Like, I should have been getting these kinds of orgasms from men for the last twenty years and no one has even come close. It's made me even more determined to create my business. Women deserve pleasure. Hell, we *need* pleasure. It's good for our brains and our bodies."

"Cheers to that," she raises her glass to me. "You're essentially a humanitarian. Fighting the good fight." She laughs and I do too.

"But with a healthy profit margin," I remind her.

"Oh, I don't doubt it for a second. And I'll be your happiest investor. I believe in you and that sex magic you've got running through your veins right now. And hurry up, because I'm ready to try anything that makes me eat chocolate cake like it's the last man on the planet, or last *men* on the planet in your case." She cocks an eyebrow at me, clearly still entertained that her buttoned-up bestie is getting with three guys at the same time. I'm still pretty entertained by it, too.

When Drea gets up to go to the bathroom, I check to see if I have any notifications for a post I did in one of my favorite forums, 'Fun, Filthy, and Almost Forty'. Ridiculous name? Maybe. But I love it. And I've gained a lot of valuable insights for my company there. It's for women navigating their sex lives in their thirties. There are a ton of posts about married women who want to spice things up, which have provided great insights into what I'm trying to fulfill with my business. But there are also a lot of posts with single women like me, who are either trying to navigate the dating world or are just happy to be alone but still want their orgasms. I took a chance and posted about my current situation. I reread my post.

Hi my beautiful internet friends,

So yes, you might associate my username with the multiple posts about recommending good toys for some solo fun. That's been my sole source of orgasms in the last few years, so again, THANKS. But now I've stumbled into a bit of a unique situation. Ughhh, welllll.... No delicate way of saying this but I'm having sex with three men at the same time. Like not in the same week, or day, but literally all of them. At. The. Same. Time. Yeah, I can't quite believe it either. I was hoping someone here might be able to give some advice on how to... maximize this opportunity? Ok, yes, I'm asking for advice taking all the peen in all the holes...

With Love, 3 Peen Queen

I giggle rereading it because I can't quite believe that this is my life and I'm the one who posted it. I scroll down to see the new comments.

> HUNGRYHUNNY117: Girl, no advice, but how does it feel living out my fantasy? Like, literally, do us a solid and describe in detail how it feels, please.

> SLUTFORDADBODS: Ummmmmm, someone is about to be d-o-u-b-l-e p-e-n-e-t-r-a-t-e-d. Yeah, it was necessary for me to spell it out like this because I think you need to really take a moment to appreciate this monumental milestone in your life. You will have two, maybe even three, penises in your body. You are out there spreading the good name of thirty-year-olds and doing this thread proud. Go! Get! Railed!

> LIBERATEDLIBIDO69: Ok, so I may or may not have some experience in this department (Okay, I definitely do, thanks to a magical summer 10 years ago that I spent on a sustainable agriculture farm in

Maine. Turns out that demographic is freaky!). Lube is your friend here. Not sure how much experience you have with butt stuff, but make sure you like that first. My favorite position is on one lap (forward or backward) on an elevated surface, so the other person can stand and enter you from the other side. Wow, never thought this information would be beneficial to anyone but me. But I hope this helps. I suddenly feel the urge to request some vacation time this summer to go see how that farm in Maine is doing...

I swallow hard and squirm in my chair. Just the thought of doing this makes me feel so incredibly hot... and excited. When I started to try to learn about my own sexuality, I also started to experiment with well, butt stuff. I wanted to see if I liked it using toys, and I do. I've never done it with anyone before because, before the Sweets, I've never even had a guy treat my vagina with much generosity, so I wouldn't dare trust them with something more complicated. But it's been something in the back of my mind that I've been craving for a very long time. And the way the Sweets make love, or *fuck*, I should say. Well, I trust them.

I switch over to my text messages and open up my group chat with the Sweets. Our normal back and forth about due dates and responsibilities is looking very different these days. The last text is from Ben.

Ben: We want to see you tonight.

He sent it three hours ago, and I didn't respond because I was on my way to meet Drea. But she'll be heading home after we get the bill and I have no plans. I decide to try a new approach for asking for what we each want because I really do want them to communicate their desires. Since they didn't ask for anything in person, it might be easier to do it over text.

> *Emily:* I want to see you guys, too. But first, I want you to tell me something that would turn you on to do during sex. I shared mine, so it's only fair.

Immediately I see typing bubbles. I smile, sensing they're just as eager as I am.

> *Deacon:* I want you to see you so thoroughly fucked and in pleasure that you forget everything else but our cocks.

My cheeks heat and I steady myself against the table.

> *Graham:* I want to come inside you.

Oh my. I want that too. So badly.

> *Ben:* I want to record you taking all three of us. Only if you feel comfortable, of course. I could hide your face. I just think it would be so sexy to show you how fucking hot you are with all of our cocks.

I can feel my underwear soak through. I am so damn excited for them I'm practically drooling.

> *Ben:* And you, Em? Tell us what you want.
>
> *Emily:* I want everything you guys just listed.
>
> *Ben:* And what else? Just ask and it's yours.

* * *

I take a deep breath. My hands are shaking as I type into my phone.

> *Emily:* I want to try to take all three of you in me at the same time. Would you be okay with that?

My heart races as the screen is still. No typing dots or anything. I start to feel nauseous, thinking I've asked for too much, that I'm too greedy.

> *Graham*: Share your location with us right now.

> *Ben:* You're so fucking hot.

> *Deacon:* We're going to give you exactly what you want, Foxy. Get ready to be thoroughly filled with Sweet dick.

CHAPTER TWELVE
Emily

By the time we get to their penthouse, they've already gotten my jacket off and somehow my bra unhooked under my dress. They must be more nimble than me because I've been trying to get at least one belt off this whole time and have failed.

Hands are everywhere and if I feel their cocks press up against me with the barrier of fabric one more time, I'm going to lose it.

"How long is this damn elevator?" I huff out as Deacon slams his lips down my chest, kissing me over the fabric of my dress.

"Too fucking long," he groans.

Finally, the elevator dings, signaling we've made it to the penthouse of their sky-rise apartment building. I've been here quite a few times but only to study. I know the elevator opens right up into their apartment and I seriously consider sprinting to one of their beds, but I've never even been to their bedrooms. Luckily, I don't have to worry about that because Ben scoops me up into his arms and carries me.

We find our way to a bedroom and Ben drops me on the giant fluffy bed, his large silhouette framed by the lights of Manhattan glowing through the giant floor-to-ceiling windows.

"Fuck," he groans. "Ms. Miller in my bed."

"Here I am." I stretch my body out on his silky blue comforter as Deacon and Graham settle next to him, watching me. "Now get yourselves naked."

Hands are everywhere. Their hands fumbling with the fabric of my dress and my hands grasping at their belt buckles.

"Did you mean it?" I say breathlessly. "About not using a condom? I'm on birth control and I've been tested."

"We're good, too." Deacon nods enthusiastically. "Are you sure about it? You want our cocks in you bare?"

I hum in delight at his words. "I want that so badly," I pant as I finally push Deacon's pants down.

"I've never been with a woman without a condom before," Deacon nips at my nipple that he just exposed. "You'll be my first Ms. Fox. The first time I feel any woman's pussy clench around me bare."

"Oh god," I say. "I can't wait another second for that." I shimmy my underwear down. "I want to feel it right now."

Deacon pulls his boxer briefs off and throws them blindly away from us, his eyes only locked on me. "Fuck yes, I can do that for you."

He straddles me, his body pinning me under him as he's perched on his own heels. The muscles of his thighs and torso flex in this position and his hard, thick cock bobs above my entrance. I'm at his mercy and I wouldn't want it any other way.

He takes his cock in his hand and then flattens it against my slit, sliding it up and down coating himself in my juices and creating delicious pressure on my clit.

I arch my back, already drunk with lust.

"My cock is meant to be covered in you," Deacon says darkly. "You're like a fucking drug."

I look up at his elegant features, twisted in need.

"Take me, Deacon. Fuck me bare. Come in me." I beg him because I need it. I need it so badly.

"God damn it, Emily." He says, gritting his teeth. Finally, he pulls my hips up and he pushes his thick length into me. Feeling his bare cock fill me up is so incredible that my body shudders and threatens an orgasm already.

"Fuck, Em. I can feel your pussy gripping me," he pumps in harder now.

I close my eyes and feel a warmth spread over my nipples. Ben and Graham are on either side of me, licking and sucking at my breasts.

I squeal. "Fuck," I sigh. "I'm already almost there. I can't hold it in."

Deacon lowers his thumb to my clit and starts massaging me and I break, my first orgasm ripping through me.

"Damn it," Deacon pulls out of me in a hurry. "I'm going to come so hard with your pussy trying to milk me like that. Graham, take over."

Graham doesn't need to be asked twice. He grabs my hips from Deacon and pushes into me just as my first orgasm is cresting. He slams into me with more roughness.

"Keep coming for me, baby. I can feel you coming on my cock." He raises my legs above me by the ankles. I yell out at the sensation. I'm so fucking full of him and can feel everything.

When my body stops quaking, Graham pulls out of me.

"Let's see how many times we can make you come," he says with a devilish smile. "I'm hoping at least three times. One for each of our cocks."

"Oh my god," I inhale. "Is that even possible?"

"One way to find out." Graham grabs my side and then flips me on my stomach. "Now let's get to this little craving of yours."

He grabs my ass cheeks and then spreads me. I gasp at being exposed like this, but also how forbidden it feels. He runs a finger from my slit to my ass, swirling my wetness around the forbidden entrance.

"Have you ever had anyone in this round ass?" He asks, pressing his finger harder against the tight entrance.

"No," I shake my head against the covers. "But I've experimented with myself."

"Experimented with yourself," Deacon's voice sounds hungry. "Go on."

"I wanted to see if I would like it, so I've put dildos up there."

"And did you? Like it?"

"Yes," I nod. "But I want the real thing. I want you."

"Mm," Ben grabs my face to look up at him, but all I can pay attention to is his enormous cock in front of me. "So after our study sessions, you would go home and fuck your own ass with a dildo? Did you ever think of us?"

I get up on my hands and knees and grab Ben's beautiful veiny cock and give it one lick around the tip. "Every," I say before bobbing my mouth deeper on his cock. "Single." I suck and then release. "Time."

CHAPTER THIRTEEN
Graham

Emily's back is arched and her ass is spread open, asking to be fucked. Have I fucking died and gone to heaven? This woman has unlocked desires so intense in me that I feel more alive than I've ever known possible. I want to claim everything about her. Every hole, every thought, every orgasm, every laugh. But right now, I'll settle for her pretty puckered ass.

I bend down and lick, devouring her from clit to asshole. I need her to come hard and deep for us again and by the way her body is responding, she's already getting there. She's squirming in pleasure as she hungrily sucks on Ben's cock.

Deacon hands me the lube we bought for this very occasion. I want her to feel fucking amazing, so I'm not taking any chances with her ass.

I warm the lube in my hands and then bring it to her ass, massaging and teasing her. I slip one finger inside her tight ass, watching her reaction. She moans and moves her hips back, greedy for more.

Fuck.

I slather the lube on my throbbing erection and line my tip

up to her asshole. I push the tip in and bite down hard, holding onto every ounce of restraint and pleasure.

I stroke myself in slowly and I hear her moan.

"That's it, baby," I grit out. "You look so fucking hot taking my cock in your ass. Do you like it?"

She nods and whimpers. I sink in deeper and her nods get more frantic. I fucking love seeing her speared in between our cocks like this and how much she wants it.

I push in, starting a rhythm and she cries, gasping as Ben pulls out of her mouth.

"Yes! I feel so full of you." She shudders. "Yes!"

I reach around and push the base of my palm into her clit, rubbing back and forth.

"I'm coming, again." She shouts. Ben lifts her up while I'm still in her, pulling her into his arms as she shakes.

I pull out of her and bite my lip hard, fighting every nerve that is begging me to come in her ass right now. The guys and I have something special planned for her final orgasm, and I will not be the one to fuck it up.

"We're not done with you, yet," Ben says in between kisses all down her neck and tits.

"Oh god," she sighs in exasperation, but she's already kissing Ben's shoulders and bringing him closer.

"Come here," I pull her tight against me. "We're going to give you what you asked for. You can take it."

I sit on the edge of the bed and pull her legs around me. I hold her face, wet and red from already being fucked everywhere, and I pepper it with kisses.

"Now, I need you to ride me," I command her. "Are you up for that?"

She nods and braces herself with my shoulders, lifting onto my cock. I hiss at the feeling of being inside her pussy again with no condom. I want to fucking live the rest of my life like this. Bury me like this.

She coaxes my entire cock inside her and grinds. She closes her eyes and mutters a low hum, gyrating more intensely and lifting her body up and down my length as she gets more into it. I lay back on the bed and let her ride my cock, finding her rhythm.

"How is it possible that all three of you feel so fucking good inside me? Better than anything I've ever felt?" She's really getting into it now, fucking me while I lay back and watch those beautiful full tits bounce. I love how comfortable she is with us now, too lost in pleasure to care about anything else.

Ben steps behind her and sucks at her neck. And Deacon gets up on the bed on his knees.

"I wonder the same thing about you," Deacon says, stroking her hair.

She takes him greedily into her mouth and I watch as she rides me and slobbers all over Deacon's dick.

"For this to work," she says in between sucks, not even willing to stop for more than a second. "I'm going to need you to fuck my mouth, Deacon."

We both groan, not expecting her to say that.

"I can make that sacrifice, Foxy," he says through a clenched jaw.

She drops her hand and stops trying to maneuver him. In response, he wraps his fingers through her hair, pushing her head down his length. She moans in encouragement.

"You ready to be fucking airtight, Ms. Miller?" Ben's voice sounds strained as he swirls the tip of his cock around her asshole.

She nods and whimpers in excitement.

I lock my eyes on her expression as she moans in ecstasy when Ben sinks into her. She claws into my chest as I thrust deeper into her and Deacon pushes himself down her throat.

We pull away and push back in like a goddamn depraved

dance, and she loves every second of it.

Ben takes his phone out just like we all agreed and films our cocks going in and out of her. I see her face twist in even more pleasure at the realization this is being captured forever for us to enjoy.

"You look so fucking sexy," he says, holding the camera to her ass. "So full of our cocks. You're taking it like a goddamn queen."

"I'm going to come," she cries out before Deacon shoves himself down her throat again.

We look at each other. This is fucking go time. Ben throws the phone down.

"Come for us, baby." I growl into her ear. "And we're going to fill you to the fucking brim with our come."

She whimpers and starts shaking. I lose it, feeling her pussy suctioning my cock, suctioning my come out of me. I explode inside of her and see goddamn stars. I watch as rope after rope of Deacon's release coats her mouth and chest and Ben's body freezes, thrusted deep and coming into her ass.

Emily's entire body is shaking, and she collapses into my chest where I hold her as her hips buck again and again on my cock until every last drop is out of me and in her. I can feel her juices soaking down between my legs as finally her body calms down.

Ben collapses down on the bed next to us and Deacon sinks to the floor.

We fucking did it. Coming at the same time was probably the most ambitious plan we've ever executed together and that includes every single grad school project. But we fucking did it.

I start to laugh, in awe. Emily starts chuckling too. Deacon and Ben join in. The four of us have lost our damn minds. And if losing my sanity feels like this fucking good, then I never want it back.

Finding Her Sweet Spots

CHAPTER FOURTEEN
Deacon

I look at the pan in amazement. The pancake actually seems to look somewhat like a pancake. But what the hell do I do now?

"How do I know when it's done?" I whisper to Graham. He's smart, he should know these things.

"How the hell should I know?" He whispers back. Okay, I take that back. Not that kind of smart.

"Shit," I curse as I flip the pancake off the pan. "Why has no one ever taught us how to cook?" I mutter angrily.

"You know I can hear you, right?" Emily laughs from where she is curled up in our leather armchair, sipping coffee and looking like a dream. She stands up and stretches long, my Knicks t-shirt rising high enough to show the lacy pink underwear she's wearing, noticeably different from last night because this woman is always prepared and, of course, she brought a fresh pair of underwear. She's the kind of competent person who probably can't believe that three grown men don't know how to cook a damn thing.

"Are you pretending to know how to cook for me?" She

grins, walking over to us. I love seeing her like this in our apartment, relaxed and thoroughly fucked rather than pounding late-night coffees to get our work done so she can quickly leave.

"We know how to cook." Ben pushes his hair back defensively. "We're sophisticated and know how to do everything an older man might know how to do."

She laughs a loud, open laugh and I savor the sound. "I've known plenty of men who couldn't cook a damn thing and had a few decades on you. It's just nice that you're trying." She comes next to me and scootches me over with her hip, taking the pancake batter from me.

"Here, I'll show you." She drops a slab of butter on the pan and then pours the batter. "When it starts bubbling, then you know it's time to flip it. Then it's almost cooked. Just get a nice brown on the other side and you're good."

"Okay, and what if for example, three hypothetical brothers might prefer blueberry pancakes? When would they put the blueberries in?" I signal to the blueberries I have uselessly sitting on the counter.

She grins, "Blueberry pancakes are my favorite, too. You're in luck, you can just plop them in right now."

I do as I'm told and drop them in. When I look up, she's staring at me with an expression I can't quite pinpoint.

"Yes, Foxy?"

"Your parents never cooked pancakes with you?"

I shrug. "Not the pancake types, I suppose. Or the cooking types at all. I'm not sure they know how to use ingredients for something other than a cocktail."

"Hm," she looks down into her coffee.

"*Yes*, Foxy?" I repeat myself.

"Well, pancakes are delicious, but it's really the idea of pancakes that makes them wonderful. It's like a celebration that you have a long morning to spend together."

"I want that, you know." I look her right in the eye. "I want to spend my life with someone who looks forward to having the morning off with me. And if I ever have kids, I'm going to make damn sure they wake up to the smell of blueberry pancakes."

She swallows hard. "That sounds nice." Her voice is smaller now, afraid. What is she so goddamn afraid of? That it could be her? Is that such a scary thought? We spend as much time as people can spend together, and it works. It works so damn well. And now the way our bodies work together... It just makes sense.

"But?" I encourage her to say more.

"Well, I was lucky, I guess. I grew up with pancake mornings when it was possible. But sometimes it wasn't that we lacked time, but money. There were six mouths to feed. There were plenty of times I didn't eat breakfast at all, so I could make sure the littlest ones ate."

"Can't you have both? Money and love?" Ben interjects from the table. "Is that so impossible?"

I know what we're talking about now goes so far beyond pancake mornings.

"I'd like to think so," she turns to Graham and Ben. "But I don't know. It seems like none of us in this room have had both." She flips the pancake off the pan and I go to make the next one, pouring the batter into the sizzling butter.

"But I've worked my whole life to get the part that I didn't have," she continues. "The money part is what I've always felt like I've had to prove. And now I'm taking the biggest risk of my life. It was crazy of me to leave my job on Wall Street to pursue my dreams. My family doesn't pursue *dreams*. We pursue stability. If I fail, all my savings are gone. And I've had to help my parents out with a lot of unexpected medical bills. They have no one else but me when things go wrong. And I have no one. So yeah, my only focus right now is the money part."

"You have us," I offer. "If you need anything, you can come to us."

She has a sad smile on her face when she turns back to me. "Deacon, that's so nice. But you know I never would in a million years. This is something I need to do on my own."

She sighs. "I guess this is all to say that one day, I'm going to need the reminder to take a step back and enjoy a pancake morning. And I hope by that time, it's not too late. But right now, all I can think about is how to make sure I can afford the ingredients for the rest of my damn life while somehow being one of those unicorns who likes what they work on."

"Hence our expiration date," Graham says dryly, clearly hating the thing as much as I do.

"Well, yeah. But I want pancake mornings in my future." She says pleadingly, "I want it all. Am I the greediest person on earth?"

"You're very good at being greedy." I get behind her and pull her into me. "We've established that already."

"Mm," she throws her head back against my chest.

"And since we're working on a deadline," I kiss down her neck. "You're going to get really good at being stuffed over and over again and still asking for more. You'll get even more greedy." I press my erection into her lower back.

Her lips part as she inhales sharply. "And you?" She whispers. "What are you greedy for?"

What I don't admit is that I'm greedy, just like her. But what I want would scare the hell out of her. I want to take over our family company with my brothers just like I want to take over her with them. I want her mind, her heart, her pussy. I want to wake up to her, go to sleep next to her, and I want to conquer the damn world with her.

But right now, she's only giving me absolute claim over one part of her. And I'll fucking take it.

I lift her up on the kitchen counter and wrap her legs around me then slip my fingers into the part of her that she has no problem giving to me. She's wet and ready for me, as always.

I pulse my fingers inside her and finally answer. "This. I'm greedy for this."

CHAPTER FIFTEEN
Emily

"Happy Expiration Date Day," I smile nervously as Graham, Deacon, and Ben grumble in my bed. It's always hilarious when they sleep over here because even though I have a big bed, we don't fit at all. But I like it because then I get to cuddle with all three of them instead of them going to their separate beds when we're at their apartment. I know they secretly like it too.

I place a tray of coffee and bagels on the bench at the foot of my bed. I watch as they slowly wake up and I attempt to burn this image into my brain before it's gone forever, their three muscled bodies flexing and stretching in my little room, waking up from a deep post-orgasmic night's sleep.

Deacon sits up to look around and then at me. "What's happy about breaking up and being woken up at the same time?" He grumbles.

"Well, technically, it's not a break-up because we're not dating." I try to keep smiling, even if I'm not really feeling like it.

"Are you gaslighting me right now, Foxy?" He says,

grabbing a bagel and tearing it open. "At least you feed your sex slaves."

I would laugh if I knew it wasn't possibly the last time Deacon would throw one if his clever retorts at me while being shirtless. I'm trying to remain cheerful. This is what we agreed on. Hell, it's what I need. I planned it so that I have my first investor pitch in two days. I don't have time to wallow. I have a million things to do.

"You guys know it's for the best. We're distracted. Our GPAs have fallen, just like I figured they would."

"Your GPA is still almost perfect," Graham says while rubbing his eyes, his hair mussed from sleep.

"It fell by .01." I point out.

"You're telling me that's not worth learning you can orgasm three times in a row?" Ben shoots up, already ready to argue, and goes straight for the coffee.

"It's been 100% worth it." I agree with him. "But now we're moving to the stage of our lives where .01% can be the difference between everything."

"Well, I have 100% of a boner right now, so I'm holding onto the .01% chance that I can keep up our Sunday tradition and sink it into you." Deacon generously gives me one more shirtless quip.

I take a deep breath, reminding myself of my fortitude. We had a full-out sex Olympics yesterday knowing that today is the end. Every step to the bagel shop reminded me of how sore and thoroughly orgasmed I am, but somehow, I still want more from them. I don't think I could ever have enough of them.

"It's not a breakup because if you were my boyfriends, then I could never in a million years break up with you guys. That's why I never agreed to anything more." I sigh, admitting the full truth. I don't feel the need to hide anything from them. "I mean really, I've thought about it and it's kind of scary what you three would have to do to make me not want you. Even if you killed a guy I would be like, ugh, well he must have had it coming…"

"He probably did." Ben takes a sip of coffee. "And that's because you trust us. The most fucking important thing, Emily, and we have it. We're unstoppable."

"I know." I nod in agreement. He's right. We are so open and clear with each other. It's the only way an arrangement like this could even exist. "But I need to grow my foundation for myself right now. Without all this sex mist all over me. And if you guys still want me-"

"We will," Ben interrupts.

"Okay," I nod. I believe him. "Then keep a space for me in your lives. And I'll do the same." I look at their faces deliberating. They're some of the most ambitious and level-headed people I know. They need this, too. "You guys know I'm right."

"It's what I love about you," Graham whispers and averts eye contact with me.

I feel my eyes heat. "We can do this," I say through a tight throat. I'm talking about this thing we have and I'm also talking about our futures. We have so much we want to achieve. It's what drove us together in the first place, our ambition and our drive.

"We got you something." Graham rubs his hand over his face before pushing himself out of my bed. He rustles through his pants that were thrown over my reading chair almost 24 hours ago. I smile, realizing he's just been naked in my apartment for almost a full day.

He pulls out a small box and I frown. "No, you guys didn't need to get me anything." I feel my heart race. We had a plan. I need them to stick to the plan. Whatever is in that small jewelry box…

"You can relax," he laughs, seeing my face. "It's not an

engagement ring. We're not that big of assholes to propose to you when you're asking for space."

He gets down on one knee. "But I can still get down on one knee to watch you freak out."

I do freak out seeing him like this. Because if it was a ring in that box, I don't think there would be even one version of myself that could say no.

I slap him on the shoulder and try to pull him up to his feet. He lumbers up with exaggerated slowness.

"Fine," he grins. "Turn around."

I do as he says, and he clears my hair to one side. Ben and Deacon stroll in front of me while Graham loops a dainty chain around my neck.

I look down and am confused at first, trying to figure out what I'm looking at.

"You like it?" Ben asks grinning.

I laugh, finally realizing what I'm looking at. The charm on the necklace is a golden stack of three pancakes, a slab of butter melting on top. There are little blue stones inlaid in it for blueberries. "Oh my gosh," I laugh again. "I love it!"

Graham steps in front of me, smiling widely. "We wanted to give it to you to remind you of what's waiting for you. We know better than anyone that all the money in the world is no good unless you have someone to spend the time with enjoying it."

Now the little misty bits in my eyes are full tears. "You guys hurry up and get what you need to get done," I say. "Because you know I work efficiently. And I'm already craving blueberry pancakes."

"Oh, Ms. Miller," Deacon says. "We're going to give you the best damn ride of your life when you're finally ready for us."

And that's all we can say for now. Because anything else would break our resolve. So I lead them to the door and do one of the hardest things I've ever done in my life. I say goodbye.

CHAPTER SIXTEEN
Emily

This morning, for the first time in six months, I take my time getting to work. And it's not because I don't have anything to do. It's because I can admit to myself I need it. An almond milk cappuccino warms my hand in the fresh fall air as I step onto the Brooklyn Bridge. Everything is golden with the light of the sunrise as I walk on the bridge's pedestrian path toward our DUMBO office, the headquarters of my company Sweet Spots. I stop halfway and take a deep breath.

Our product launch was a week ago today and it went really damn well. I over-planned and undersold, anticipating some colossal disaster. But it didn't happen. And in fact, the response has been overwhelming. It turns out that a business like this gets people talking. Even the bad press about people scandalized by our concept is working in our favor.

But it wasn't the milestone I thought it would be. Instead, it's only been the beginning of more work. In fact, I could work all day and all night for the rest of my life and still have work to do. A dark anxiety rushed over me after the launch and that's when I made a realization. The only people I would want to talk about this feeling with are Graham, Ben, and Deacon. I want to talk about the bad stuff and I want to celebrate the good stuff with them. I wasn't expecting that.

So after a lot of nervous pacing and working up the nerve, I finally made an appointment with their secretary to see them later today. I'm using this walk to work to gather my thoughts on just what I want to say to them.

Don't get me wrong, I'm extremely proud of myself. Even though to some people, it might seem like I don't have my priorities straight. Lord knows my father can't get over the fact that I've spent my late 30s growing a company rather than a baby. But luckily he has no say in my happiness anymore. That's the beautiful thing about getting older. You realize that at the end of the day, caring what others think is the worst reason to stop you from pursuing what you know is right for you.

I take a deep sigh. The important part is knowing what is right for you, though. I worry I made the biggest mistake of my life cutting the Sweets out. They didn't need the extra ten years it took me to figure out what I wanted. They knew. And part of what they wanted was me. And I treated them like garbage because I couldn't admit to myself that I want them too. Technically, yes, I can do this life alone. I've proved that to myself now. But I *want* to do this life with them.

Of course, I've read about them in the news. It's hard to miss one of the greatest hostile takeovers of a company in history. After we graduated, they were able to oust their own father with a vote of no confidence. I was dying to call them up and see if they were okay. Even though their father seems like an awful man, it couldn't have been easy doing that. But they're not mine to call up anymore. I made sure of that six months ago.

I start walking again, trying to rid myself of the nasty thoughts that inevitably start up right about now. That I chose work over love. That I've lost the three most important men in my life. That I'll never be held by them again, the one thing I crave every night before I fall asleep.

I take the elevator up to our office and the dark red logo in neon over the reception desk greets me. Personal time is over, I remind myself. It's time to get my head back in the game. But it doesn't come easily to me today.

"Good morning, Emily!" Our receptionist, Willa, says cheerfully to me. "You have a meeting waiting for you in the Blush Conference Room."

I cock my head in confusion. I didn't have any meetings on my calendar. I pull my phone out to text Drea, as my largest investor, she's the only person allowed to make appointments without consulting me first. But before I can, I spot a silhouette moving in the Blush Conference Room. And then another. And another. It's three outlines that are imprinted on my brain and into my skin. I feel my lips wet simply from processing the information that they're nearby.

"Sweet Spots is doing so well, we've come to apply for open positions," Deacon's voice is rich velvet to my ears. I want to just melt into a puddle on the floor seeing the three of them. I do my best to stop myself from taking a deep inhale to take in the same scent that is so intrinsically woven with pleasure and joy. They're the same guys I know but they look slightly different. Their haircuts are closer cut and they're dressed in tailored suits instead of the more casual outfits they wore to school.

"Oh?" I play along. "And what qualifications would you like to bring to the company?"

"We have hands-on practical experience at aiding the CEO, including operating her squirt function." Deacon jokes like no time has passed.

A laugh breaks open my chest and cuts away at the nerves of seeing them again. Of course, a million thoughts are going through my head, but mostly one big one over and over. *Do they still want me? Do they still want me? Do they still want me?*

"We've loved watching you make your dreams come true." Ben smiles warmly at me. "Sure, we wanted to be by your side in case you needed us. But you did it. We always knew you could do whatever you wanted."

I swallow hard. "I thought the same. When I saw the news about the takeover, I wanted to rush over to see you guys and see if you were okay."

"We were okay," Graham speaks now. "We just missed you."

His words are like a soft touch. I let them sit for a moment and warm me, bolster me.

"I've missed you so much," I finally exhale, pure relief coursing through me. "I made an appointment with your secretary for later today so I could grovel."

"We couldn't wait the whole day to see you." Graham pulls me in against his chest and holds me there. "But feel free to grovel away."

I playfully hit him and step away. I take a deep breath. I need to look at them for what I'm about to say.

"It wasn't fair to you guys how I ended things. It was controlling and selfish and the one who lost out was me. Because last week, when I experienced one of the most surreal accomplishments of my life, I wanted to share it with you. But I couldn't because I pushed you away." I take another breath. "I'm so sorry. I don't blame you if you don't want me."

They're silent for a moment and I swear my heartbeat fills the whole room.

"We would do anything for you, Emily." Graham starts.

"We stayed away because that's what you wanted. And we knew it was the right call. I hope you never forgot that once in the last six months. We stayed away for you and we're back here for you. We want *you*."

My eyes mist. How did I get so lucky? How did I manage to have even more than I ever wanted? I think back to the scared girl I was ten years ago. I felt like life was happening to me, and I deserved the worst. Yet, now somehow, I have the best. At least the best for me. And that's the trick, isn't it? When I made that decision that I wanted to be happy, it couldn't mean anything but pursuing what was best for me specifically. That led me to business school, a bit of an unconventional business idea, and now the *very* unconventional loves of my life. And that's what they are. The loves of my life. I know it in my head, my heart, deep into my bones, and definitely between my legs.

But I also need to make sure I am the best for them. "I've considered myself only for so long," I say. "Tell me how I can be the best for you."

Ben pulls me into a kiss first. Deacon comes up behind me and grabs my waist and turns me around to kiss him. And then Graham. We're back together and it feels so right.

"The best for us is that you take today off and make a new contract with us," Deacon says.

"A new contract, huh? What does it entail?"

"No end date and lots of sex."

"I'll text my assistant right now," I grab at them to hustle out the door. Today I'm choosing a blueberry pancake morning. Actually, screw that, I'm choosing a blueberry pancake life. The sweetest kind there is.

CHAPTER SEVENTEEN
Epilogue

One Year Later

Graham

"Now tell me, gorgeous," Meg refills Emily's whiskey glass. "Which one is the best at cunnilingus? My money is on Graham. It's always the more reserved ones who just eat it up like a meal."

"Hey, cheers, Meg." I raise my glass to Meg, her bright red hair making her an easy target to find despite all the whiskies I've had. "I appreciate that."

"You don't have to answer that," Ben laughs.

"Oh, man Meg," Emily says with buzzed enthusiasm. "You're so right. Graham is an absolute freak in bed." She stops and knits her brows together. "But I guess they all are." Then she starts laughing hysterically. "And I guess that makes me one, too."

Meg did a great job of getting our Em wasted tonight. She's been trying for a year since we first brought her to The

Whiskey Drop, but tonight is the first time she actually succeeded.

"Okay, Foxy," Deacon is laughing now, too. "It is time to get you home."

"Home!" Emily raises a finger in the air like she's about to recite a monologue. "Our home! Meg, have I told you we moved in together? It's the best thing ever."

"Only about 100 times tonight, love," Meg says winking at me.

"You did this." I mouth silently at her and she just shrugs, laughing.

We pile into an extra-large cab and I pull Emily in the back with me, coaxing her head onto my lap in case she wants to sleep. At first, she cuddles into my lap and closes her eyes, but then they shoot open.

"Oh!" She exclaims. "I'm going to check Sweet Spots for any new positions we can try tonight."

"Tomorrow," I correct her. "You have about five shots of whiskey you need to sleep off."

"Do I?" She asks with a sleepy yawn. "Fine then, tomorrow." She scrolls through the app. She's been so good at keeping her work life at work. It was something she was worried about when we gave this thing a real try a year ago. Sure, there are late nights spent working for all of us. That's unavoidable. But when we're together, we're really together. Even if right now she's scrolling through her phone and giggling, I know it will benefit both of us tomorrow. Sweet Spots has paid off in many ways.

"What's so funny?" I run my thumb along her smile that's lit up by the blue phone screen.

"Someone suggested that we do a taste test. Like you put different foods on your cocks and I need to guess the food and also guess the cock. Honestly, it would be a real challenge because you're all so similar in size. I think I might get more feedback based on the foods you would choose."

"I think we definitely should test that theory tomorrow morning," Deacon chimes in.

Em giggles again. It's almost too damn sweet to handle. We've got such a good thing going. It's why tonight, our first night in our new home, was going to be a special occasion. But then Meg went and got us all wasted, so now we need a new plan.

"Oh my god," Emily sits up. "Oh you guys, this is amazing."

"What?" We all answer in a drunk Sweet brothers chorus.

"So you know how I gave everyone on my favorite forum lifetime access to Sweet Spots?"

"The forum that gave you advice on how to take all three of our cocks at once? Hell, I'd get them a lifetime subscription to anything," Ben chimes in from the front.

"Exactly. Well, one of the women posted on the new Sweet Spots' 'Fun & Filthy' forum. I have to read it to you."

She clears her throat.

> Thank god for this thread because I am absolutely not telling any single person that I have to look in the eyes this… And please don't judge me, because I'm in a fuck-it-all-burn-it-to-the-ground phase of my life thanks to my asshole ex. Which brings me to the fact that I might be sleeping with three men at the same time. I was hired to teach them etiquette. But they're the ones teaching me that I like some truly filthy, dirty things. (Remember when I said no judgment??) Someone tell me I'm not crazy for wanting three guys in their 20s? Someone tell me I won't regret this and I deserve some orgasms too? Maybe someone tell me how the hell I'm supposed to satisfy three cocky shitheads that are appallingly sexy?

Please help. Xoxo, Miss Training Tramp

"Give her all the advice, baby." Ben laughs while reaching to the back seat to grab Emily's hand.

"Tell her how to tame those young studs," Deacon adds, and I wonder what the hell the cab driver is thinking we're in the business of by the time he pulls outside our new brownstone to drop us off.

"Don't fuck it up," I growl at Deacon as he pours the batter on the cast iron pan. It's our first breakfast in our new home. But it's so much more than that.

"Damn, Graham. Didn't you pay attention in management class? Fear is not a sustainable motivator." Deacon shoots back.

"I'm not looking for longevity, but perfection," I say as I get back to setting the table. Ben is currently responsible for keeping Emily in bed a little longer and hopefully making sure she's not too hungover.

I take a step back as Deacon brings the first batch of pancakes and puts it on our long oak table. We've learned how to do pancakes, bacon, omelets, and a mean fucking cup of coffee. Long Saturday brunches have become our favorite tradition and having it in our own home together is a better reality than I ever could have imagined for myself. Fuck, I didn't know life could feel this good. It never felt like this growing up. None of the damn warm fuzzies I get all the fucking time now when I just sit back and watch Emily bantering with my brothers and think, "How the hell did we get so lucky?".

"Oh, this smells good!" Emily comes charging down the

stairs and Ben just shrugs at us behind her. He's lucky we finished early.

"You guys," she stops with a huge smile on her face. "Our first Saturday brunch in our own home together. Is this real life?"

"How are you feeling?" I pull her into me for a hug.

"Surprisingly, okay. I think whiskey agrees with me." She shrugs.

"Well, that's convenient because we love whiskey and we love you." I kiss the top of her head, but she leans up to take my lips. She slips her hand under my shirt and along the ridges of my stomach.

"I love you guys. And I would also love to try that little game I mentioned last night." She pulls me by the fabric of my shirt and sits me down, jumping on my lap and straddling me. "How would the technicalities work out? I mean we have this big spread. You could find something here to put on your cocks while I-"

"Em," I laugh. "Em, we'll have time for that."

She pulls back, looking suspicious. Probably because I've never once denied her any of her kinky ideas and hell, I don't want to right now either. But I'm not about to let our plans be delayed again.

"Foxy, why don't you serve yourself some breakfast?" Deacon helpfully suggests.

She stands up, looking at us all as if we've sprouted extra heads.

Deacon laughs. "Is this how rarely we refuse our Foxy's luscious demands?" He pulls her in for a sensual kiss and she presses herself into him. "That only one time we say we'll fuck after breakfast instead of before, you think there's something wrong?"

He pulls her away from him and turns her toward the table and then smacks her on the ass.

"Well, yes." She shrugs. "I think I'm the best fucked woman in Manhattan. Maybe the world." She sits down in her spot and opens up her cloth napkin. "I mean I don't think I've had to touch myself for-" She shakes her cloth napkin and a box falls out, clinking onto the table

"What is this?" She says slowly as her glare shifts to each one of us.

We surround her, getting on one knee.

"No!" She shouts, tears filling her eyes.

"Is that your answer?" Ben teases her.

She opens up the box. Three diamonds shine on a platinum band that's been custom-made for her.

"Yes!" She shouts. "I mean, my answer is yes! Of course!"

She stands up so her chair flies out behind her and jumps into my arms. I catch her and nestle my nose into her neck, inhaling her and imprinting this memory to keep forever.

Deacon and Ben come up behind her and embrace her. She turns between us, giving us each hugs which turn into intense and tear-filled kisses.

"Forget the game for now," she says, still through tears. "I want to make good old-fashioned love to my fiancés."

"Nothing about us will ever be old-fashioned," I pull her tighter against me, showing her just how hard I am for her. "But we've got a lot of love to give you."

She grinds against me.

"Bedroom, now." She demands.

"Wait," Ben pulls away. "You don't even have the ring on yet."

"Oh," she laughs. "Right. I just got so excited."

Ben grabs the box and gets down on his knee and slips it on her finger. Perfect fit.

She holds it out and admires it. "It's perfect. A diamond for each of you."

"Perfect, like you." Deacon grabs her ass and pulls her into him. "*Ms. Sweet.*"

Want to find out what happens to Miss Training Tramp on the Fun & Filthy Forums? Her steamy and satisfying story, **Taming Her Temptations** *is out now!*

Sign up for **Joya's Joyful Updates** to be the first to know about it: bit.ly/34ajqt7

Thank you so much for reading *Finding Her Sweet Spots*! If you enjoyed this book, a review is the nicest thing in the world. Thank you!

About the Author

Joya Lively loves pleasure. Especially when it comes in the form of gorgeous men. Throw in some humor and an excited heroine and you've just described a perfect Saturday morning.

She writes stories that are all about making the heroine feel good, in more ways than one. She has a special soft spot for tales where the heroes and heroines feel safe and empowered to explore their deepest desires.

If you want to escape into pages filled with insatiable and seductive characters, then you've come to the right author.

Sign up to get Joya's Joyful Updates which will give you first dibs on all new releases:
bit.ly/34ajqt7

Printed in Great Britain
by Amazon